Ambush in the Foothills

Ambush in the Foothills

Bill Freeman

James Lorimer & Company Ltd., Publishers
Toronto, 2000

James Lorimer & Company Ltd. acknowledges the support of the Ontario Arts Council for our publishing program. We acknowledge the financial support of the Government of Canada through the Book Publishing Industry Development Program (BPIDP) for our publishing activities. We acknowledge the support of the Canada Council for the Arts for our publishing program.

Cover illustration: Sharif Tarabay

Canadian Cataloguing in Publication Data

Freeman, Bill, 1938-
    Ambush in the foothills

(Bains series)
ISBN 1-55028-717-6 (bound)   ISBN 1-55028-716-8 (pbk.)

I. Title.

PS8561.R378A82 2000   jC813'.54   C00-931896-8
PZ7.F73Am 2000

James Lorimer & Company Ltd., Publishers
35 Britain Street
Toronto, Ontario
M5A 1R7

Printed and bound in Canada

The Old Chisholm Trail

Well, come along boys, and listen to my tale,
I'll tell you of my troubles on the old Chisholm Trail.

(Chorus) Come a ti yi yippy yippy yay, yippy yay.
Come a ti yi yippy yippy yay.

Oh, my foot in the stirrup and my seat in the saddle,
I'm the best cowboy that every roped cattle.

I'm up in the mornin' before daylight,
And before I sleep the moon shines bright.

I woke up one mornin' on the old Chisholm Trail,
A rope in my hand, and a cow by the tail.

Oh, it's bacon and beans most every day,
I'd as soon be eatin' prairie hay.

It's cloudy in the west and lookin' like rain,
My darned old slicker's in the wagon again.

I went to the boss to draw my roll,
He figured me out nine dollars in the hole.

A-ropin' and a-tyin' and a-brandin' all day,
I'm workin' mighty hard for mighty little pay.

So I went to the boss, and we had a little chat,
I slapped him in the face with my big slouch hat.

Oh, the boss says to me: "I'll fire you!
Not only you, but the whole darn crew."

So I sold my rope, and I sold my saddle,
'Cause I'm tired of punchin' those longhorn cattle.

I'm a-goin' back home, no jokin' or lyin',
I'm a-goin' back home, just a-yellin' and a-flyin'.

Historical Note

By the middle of the 1870s peace had come to the foothills country of Canada. The North West Mounted Police had driven out the whiskey traders who had come up the Whoop-Up Trail. The Blackfoot nation were facing a crisis with the disappearance of the buffalo, but under the leadership of Chief Crowfoot, and others, they chose the path of peace rather than war. Traders and settlers were moving into the foothills looking for new opportunities.

It was at this time that a few enterprising people decided they would try to raise cattle on the lush rolling grasslands in what we now call southern Alberta. Cattle ranching in North America had begun in Texas and gradually moved onto the northern ranges. By the 1860s large-scale ranching had already been established in western Montana. Canadians went down into Montana, bought herds, and drove them north into the foothills country. These early ranchers faced hardship, isolation and dangers, but they persevered. By the 1880s, with the arrival of the railroad, their markets expanded and they went on to establish the Alberta beef cattle industry that continues to thrive to this very day.

Ambush in the Foothills is fiction, but the adventures of Kate, Jamie, Billy and others, described in this book, are based on the experiences of people who struggled to establish ranching in Alberta. Their stories are part of the real history of the people of Canada.

Bill Freeman

1

Jamie and Kate were working in the parade square of Fort Walsh the day that Constable Patrick McNeil of the North West Mounted Police brought in the two outlaws. One was a mean-looking man in his early twenties with a permanent snarl. The other was no more than Jamie's age.

The policeman swung off his big black horse, snapped to attention and saluted the inspector. "Constable Patrick McNeil reporting, sir. I found these two selling whisky to a band of Blackfoot along a stream west of the Cypress Hills." McNeil stood ramrod straight. He was tall with dark hair and clean-shaven.

"What action did you take, constable?"

"I arrested the pair and poured their whisky out on the ground, sir."

"A waste of good whisky," the oldest of the outlaws muttered.

"Quiet!" the inspector ordered. "Do you intend to lay charges, Constable McNeil?"

"Yes, sir. Selling liquor to the natives."

"You can't do that!" The outlaw was furious. "We're Americans!"

The constable turned on him. "And this is Canada, McCoy! You have to obey our laws when you are here."

"You'll pay for this, Patrick McNeil! You'll pay!"

But no more arguments were tolerated. The red-coated policeman undid the ropes holding them, and the outlaws were marched off to jail cells.

Kate and Jamie Bains had witnessed other scenes like this in the fort. Weeks before they had intended to return to the family homestead in Manitoba, but when winter struck with its full fury, dumping snow on the barren prairie, they knew that there was no way that they could travel safely.

To ride by horseback across that tree-less, snow-filled prairie, without a landmark to show the way, would invite disaster, and the brother and sister were too wise in the ways of that wild country to even try. The fort commander, Superintendent James Walsh, offered them a place to stay and their meals in return for doing chores around the fort, and they had accepted.

The whole country had closed down. Native people huddled around fires in their teepees. Even the North West Mounted Police constables stayed in their barracks at Fort Walsh, enjoying the warmth of the big cast-iron stoves and rest from the dangerous task of bringing law and order to the raw Canadian frontier in that winter of 1876–77.

Life was good for them at the fort. The police constables were mostly young men in their twenties and full of fun. The work was not so hard. Jamie split firewood and carried water. Kate helped the cook and tidied up a bit. Her brother slept in the barracks with the men. He was fifteen now and almost as tall as the constables. Even Kate recognized that he was changing into a man.

But this was a police outpost in the middle of wild country. There always seemed to be some crisis: reports of starvation among native people, outbreaks of smallpox, worries about attacks by the Blackfoot or the Sioux. The police had much work to do.

Still, it seemed a safe place. Kate was a favourite in the isolated, male-dominated world of the North West Mounted Police fort, and she played it to her own advantage. She was a pretty thirteen-year-old with blond hair and bright eyes. The men fussed over her and always had a joke or a story for her. They had made her a cozy corner in the barracks where she gained some privacy by hanging up blankets. When she had time she liked to sit on her bed and dream and read.

It was in those cold weeks, sitting around the big stove in the barracks, that Constable Patrick McNeil explained his dream to anyone who would listen. "The Canadian foothills to the west of us will be ranching country. One day there will be thousands of head of beef cattle grazing on that land, and I intend to be a part of it."

There were some who did not believe him, but most of the policemen had been into the short-grass country around Fort Macleod, and they had seen the rich grasslands of the rolling foothills that stretched all the way to the Rocky Mountains in the West.

And who could not but be captured by the enthusiasm of the dreamer? Patrick was a man in his late twenties, with an impressive military bearing, who had proven himself over and over again to be a good police officer in difficult country. But when he talked about cattle, and the potential of the foothills country, he got a faraway look in his eye, like a man excited about the prospect of his own future.

"All you have to do is get a few head of cattle," he explained, "and they will multiply into a herd all on their own." His hands made sweeping gestures as he visualized the growth of his herd. "The animals look after themselves out on the range. Chinook winds melt the snow to give good grazing in winter. Buffalo survived for centuries on that land and so can cattle."

Jamie and Kate were drawn to Patrick's enthusiasm and generous personality. Often they sat by the hot stove as he expanded on his dream.

"I've got it all figured out down to the last penny," he explained to them one cold afternoon. "My three-year term with the mounted police is over this spring. I've gathered some money from friends in the force and my own savings. I'm going to go down into the Montana Territory, buy a herd and drive them up to the Canadian foothills. I'll be there by midsummer."

"It sounds so exciting," said Jamie in awe.

Patrick smiled to see the interest. "Why don't you come with me, Jamie? You're a good horseman. We can work together. It's a great opportunity."

"But there's Kate, and ..."

"She can come too. I need all the help I can get. It will be a great future for all of us." Again Patrick's eagerness had run away with him.

"We can't, Jamie, we have to go home to Manitoba. Our mother is expecting us," Kate insisted.

"Yes. I guess you're right, Kate." The boy looked crestfallen.

But Jamie came to share the dream of being a cattleman and a rancher. Often, in the days ahead, he found himself talking to Patrick about the prospect. Cattle ranching started in Texas, the policeman explained, and now was spreading into the northern plains of the United States. Along with the cattle came cowboys, those hardy men who tended the herds and lived their life on the open range. Inevitably, Patrick concluded, cattle and cowboys were going to come to the Canadian foothills, and he was determined to join them.

Jamie brooded over it. What about his future? His family expected him to return to Manitoba and work on the homestead. But he was a horseman, not a farmer. What he wanted more than anything else was to be out on the prairie with his horses. If he returned home, would it mean that he would have to give it all up?

Jamie was a straightforward, clear-thinking type of person, not given to brooding over impossible prospects, but

Patrick had made this dream of herds of cattle and cowboys so real it seemed easy to reach. The money to buy the herd had already been gathered together. All they had to do was go south into Montana Territory, get the cattle and drive them north into the Canadian foothills country. What could be difficult about that?

But as the winter wore on there were things around the fort for Jamie and Kate to think about, other than cattle and cowboys. One of Jamie's chores was to take food to the two prisoners that Patrick had arrested for bootlegging. When they appeared in court the magistrate had sentenced them to a month in the Fort Walsh lockup, and they were ordered out of the country when they were released.

The two prisoners made life miserable for the boy. McCoy was a loud mouth who would not let Jamie alone.

"What kind of police slop have you got for us to eat today, kid?" he would growl in a threatening voice.

After he had finished complaining about the food he would curse the country and the policeman who had arrested them. "Canada is a fool place, ruled by a Queen who lives halfway across the world and a bunch of men in red coats runnin' around like they think they're important."

"We've got our own government in Ottawa," Jamie replied, feeling honour bound to defend his country.

McCoy laughed. "What do you know, kid? If you ever go south you'll see the way a country should be run. Only just watch yourself 'cause it's every man for himself down in the United States of America. You and your redcoats would never survive."

The other prisoner, the partner of McCoy, was a boy named Billy. He was a surly, threatening kid who did not say much, but every time that McCoy gave an insult he would laugh in encouragement. Feeling Billy's eyes on him made Jamie uneasy.

"You wait 'til we get out of this jail," McCoy once said to Jamie at lunch time. "These redcoats are gonna sit up and take notice."

"You've been ordered to leave the country once you are released."

"Nobody's gonna order us around." McCoy yanked his plate of food out of Jamie's hand. "I've done lots of bad things: whisky trading, cattle rustling. I've been a wolfer and a buffalo skinner and lots else. There ain't nothin' I haven't done so you and your mounted police friends had better watch out." Once his anger had spilled out he retreated to the back of the cell to brood.

The two prisoners held a special hatred for Patrick McNeil because he had arrested them, and Jamie felt he should warn the police constable of McCoy's threats. He was with Kate when he found Patrick grooming his horse in the stables.

When Jamie related what had been said the constable stiffened into a stern policeman. "Those two have found out that in Canada there is a rule of law, not rule by outlaws." Then he softened a little and laughed in a good-humoured way. "Men like that brag and swagger about. They try and scare people. You have to ignore most of what they say."

"I'd be careful of them," warned Jamie.

"Thanks, but you don't have to worry about me. I can defend myself against bandits."

Kate still felt uneasy. "But if you travel down to Montana, there will be lots of men like that."

"Why don't you come to help defend me, Kate?" Patrick's face brightened into a broad smile.

"We've got to go home."

"What about you, Jamie?" Patrick continued. "Have you given it some thought? The two of you would be an asset on the trip. Spring is coming. In two weeks I will be discharged from the force. I'm getting my gear together, and I'll be on my way south to get a herd of cattle. You have your own horses. It'll be an easy ride. We'll be back in Canada by midsummer. You can make a little money and see some new country. What could be simpler?" Patrick's enthusiasm had swept him along. A moment later he was whistling as he went about his duties.

That night, after all of the chores were completed and the barracks had quieted, Jamie lay in his bunk as he turned Patrick's offer over in his mind. Finally he eased his feet onto the floor and crossed to his sister's corner of the room.

"Kate ... Kate ... are you awake?"

"Is that you, Jamie?"

"I need to talk to you. It's important."

The two of them snuggled under blankets on Kate's bed and whispered so no one would be disturbed. As they talked they could hear the dripping of melted snow off the barrack's roof. A chinook from the foothills had come. Spring was not far away.

"Kate, I want to go with Patrick down to Montana to get the herd of cattle," the boy announced quietly.

"But mother's expecting us home, Jamie."

"I want to work with horses and cattle. I'm talking about my future, Kate. I've always worked with horses. Even when I was back in Ontario people said I had a gift with horses. If I go with Patrick I can be with him when they first bring cattle into the foothills country, and ... and I can make a life for myself."

Jamie had always been thoughtful, and Kate knew he would have mulled this over before he talked to her about it. "But what about our mother?" she asked.

"She'll understand. We'll write a letter and explain it to her. She has John and Robbie to help her out on the farm."

"Then you want me to go with you?"

"Mother insisted that we stay together. Remember? And ... yes. I'd like you to come."

Kate turned it over in her mind. Jamie had always supported and helped her in the past. It was only fair that she support him. Patrick McNeil said that it was safe; they would be back in Canada by midsummer. And it would be good to return home with a little money to help support the family.

In Kate's hesitation Jamie sensed that she was wavering. "If it doesn't work out we'll head back home as soon as we get the cattle into Canada."

"But Mother ..."

"She trusts us, Kate. You know that. I've had to work away from home a lot and I've survived. We'll be together. We can look after each other."

There was a long silence as the two of them listened to the water drip off the roof.

Finally Kate spoke. "We've already been away from home for six months. I guess another four months won't matter that much."

2

When Patrick heard that Kate and Jamie had decided to ride with him he suddenly had second thoughts. "I'm not so sure about Kate coming with us," he told the two of them.

"What do you mean?" The young girl bristled.

"You could hold us up, and, you know, you're a girl."

"I can ride as well as any man."

It was Jamie who made the difference. "Kate's my sister, and if I go, she comes with us. You'll see. She can do her share of the work."

"Well, all right." Patrick knew he had to back down on this one. He was going to need every hand he could find if he was going to get the herd he was buying back to Canada. "But there will be hardships on the trail, and I don't want to be worried about girls. Get your horses and gear ready."

"When do we leave?" Jamie asked.

They were standing in the middle of the parade square of the fort. Patrick gazed up at the sun beating down on them from the clear blue sky. A warm springlike breeze fluttered the Union Jack at the top of the pole. The snow seemed to be melting right before their eyes.

"By the end of the week I'll have my discharge papers. If this warm weather keeps up, I want to leave the day after they are issued."

Kate knew what would be her most serious problem. She was expected to wear the long full skirts that were the fashion. But wearing a skirt made it hard to ride a horse. If she was going to be out on the trail for weeks then she needed a pair of leggings.

She hunted through a storeroom and found an old pair of riding breeches that had been discarded and tried them on. They were a little baggy and had a hole in the knee, but with a little repair they would be perfect. In her spare time she carefully mended the breeches, put them on and one afternoon wore them around the grounds of the fort.

Jamie made no comment when he saw her in her new outfit. After all he knew his sister's temperament, but the other men could not help saying things when they saw her in her breeches. The worst was Patrick. Kate and Jamie passed by him near the stables. The young constable brought them up short with his commanding, military voice.

"You're not going to be wearing that ... that man's outfit, are you?" He was looking distinctly uncomfortable.

Kate stiffened. "It's perfect for riding."

"But it's not proper. The fairer sex should wear their dresses and female things."

"Even out here on the frontier?" Kate was getting more annoyed by the moment.

"Yes, especially out here. We should be setting a standard of what is acceptable."

Jamie could barely stop laughing. Patrick McNeil had a lot to learn about his sister.

Kate's jaw thrust out stubbornly. "Well I say that these breeches are perfect for the trail. I'm going to wear them, and that's all there is to it."

"But ... but ..." Patrick was flabbergasted, but how could he resist such a willful girl? "Well if you insist then maybe it will be all right when we are out on the trail, but whenever we are around other people, or in town, you must wear your skirt and proper female things."

"Well ... all right." Kate was about to head back to the barracks when she turned on her heel and addressed the constable and her brother. "But if the two of you think that I am going to follow your bidding on this trip then you can think again." And then she stamped off.

Patrick was shaken. He thought that females should do whatever men told them to do. "When I first suggested she come I was joking, but now ..." he said almost timidly.

The boy smiled. "Kate will do more than her share. You'll see. But she makes her own mind up about things."

In their rush to get ready for the trip Jamie forgot that the prisoners would be released about the same time. He and his sister had taken their horses to the blacksmith shop to get new shoes. They were standing about watching the work when Billy, the youngest of the outlaws, suddenly appeared.

"What are you doing here?" Jamie asked uneasily.

Billy wore a broad-brimmed hat, dungarees, a plaid shirt and riding boots that came up to his knees. He carried a worn saddle over his shoulder and a Winchester rifle in the other hand. "Did you think that we escaped from that tin-pot jail?"

"Where's our horses, kid?" McCoy had appeared. He had a similar outfit as Billy but also carried a six-gun strapped to his waist.

"They're grazing outside the fort."

McCoy swore angrily. "Just like them redcoats. Least they could have done is have them ready when we were released from that flea-bitten hell hole."

Patrick heard the commotion and suddenly appeared. He stiffened into his full military bearing as he heard the complaints. "You heard the boy. Your horses are outside the fort. Get moving!"

McCoy turned on him angrily. "Why should we?"

"The magistrate ordered you out of Canada."

McCoy dropped his saddle on the ground as if preparing for a fight. "And what if we don't!"

"Then we've got some good penitentiaries where the two of you can have a nice long holiday."

"No man's gonna take away my freedom like that."

"If you want to remain free then I recommend that you get on your horse and move south fast. Understand?"

The two men stood nose to nose, glaring angrily at each other. Other mounted police officers were beginning to gather. Some carried weapons. All were deadly serious.

McCoy looked about uneasily. The odds were not in his favour. Slowly he picked up his saddle and hoisted it onto his shoulder. "We're goin'. Don't worry about that. We don't want to stay in a country ruled by a bunch of men who run around in red coats. But let me tell you this. Down in Montana we've got a different attitude about the law, and it's not friendly to people who get all stuck up with their own importance. Understand?"

McCoy and Billy walked out through the gates of the fort with a half a dozen mounted policemen watching them.

An inspector turned to Patrick. "You'd better avoid those two when you go down to the Montana Territory."

The constable stiffened. "Outlaws will never intimidate me!" And he headed off on his business.

It was three days later when Patrick's discharge papers were issued. They spent the rest of the day getting their gear together, and just before dawn the next day they saddled up and swung aboard their mounts. Patrick, dressed in civilian clothes, led the way out of the fort with Kate and Jamie riding behind.

Kate was proudly wearing her new riding breeches along with a warm canvas jacket and a black broad-brimmed hat that one of the policemen had given her. Her blond hair, tied behind her head, flowed out onto her shoulders. She felt a special thrill to be riding on such an important mission.

The fort's contingent of constables and officers were lined up for roll call in front of the barracks. The Union Jack was run up the pole as the bugle sounded. Superintendent Walsh snapped to attention and saluted the riders. "Bring those beef cattle back, Patrick," he called out after them. "Safe journey!" As the gates of the fort swung open to let them pass they heard a cheer go up from the assembled police officers.

They rode single file, following a small stream that led towards the west. The Cypress Hills rose high above them, covered in lodgepole pine. The morning was cool, but as the sun rose in the clear blue sky, the land warmed. Large pockets of snow that lay in the shade of the hills were rapidly melting, sending a thousand rivulets down towards the stream.

As they passed an Assiniboine encampment, smoke from the cooking fires gave a haze to the air. Children were playing as men prepared their horses and weapons to go on the hunt. For a moment Kate thought of their Assiniboine friends, and then she found herself thinking about home.

At this time of the morning their mother would be preparing breakfast. Robbie would be getting ready for school and John, perhaps, was feeding the livestock. They had been away from home so long now she wondered if their family thought about them anymore.

As much as she missed home Kate was still glad to be out on the trail. She felt comfortable in her outfit, and the feel of her buffalo pony moving under her gave a sense of freedom and new expectations. She looked around, taking in the beauty of this new spring day.

It was a wonderful, fresh morning, the first really warm day of the new season. The land was waking from its long winter hibernation. Birds were stirring in the trees. They saw rabbits and gophers exploring their territory, and Jamie spotted the hulking form of a black bear with a pair of young cubs up on a hillside.

Patrick set the pace at an easy canter. Soon the valley broadened and then abruptly they were out of the hills, with its pine forests, and into rolling grasslands that stretched unendingly to the west. All day they rode almost due south under the big blue sky, with the sun high overhead and a steady breeze stirring the golden brown grass. Soon green shoots would rejuvenate the land.

Patrick knew the country they were travelling through better than any white man alive. He explained that it used to be disputed territory warred over by the Blackfoot confederacy, whose territory lay to the west, and the Cree and their Assiniboine allies who lived to the east and the north. Now it was peaceful as native people struggled to find enough food to eat. They had no time or energy for war.

It was the white traders, who came up the Whoop-Up Trail from Fort Benton, who caused trouble in this territory now. Men like McCoy and Billy, who traded rot-gut whisky to the Blackfoot for buffalo hides and other furs, had impoverished the native people. The North West Mounted Police had been set up to stamp out the trade. Most of it had been accomplished, but there were still a few bad apples. Patrick had made a big contribution to the force, and he was not slow in telling Kate and Jamie about it.

There was a certain part of Patrick's personality that was pure policeman, rigid and militaristic, but there was another side of him that was like an optimistic, enthusiastic boy out for a new adventure. Many hours of the ride were whiled away with his stories of his captures of outlaws or his dealings with Blackfoot chiefs. As he told it, he was a man who had gained the respect of many since he had come into this country four years before, and he intended to accomplish a great deal more in the years ahead.

They rode all day, and by the late afternoon they had reached the banks of the Milk River. Patrick led them to a ford where the water was shallow enough for the horses to wade across. On the other side, settled on a tabletop hill overlooking the surrounding countryside, they found a small Blackfoot encampment of five teepees. When they rode up to the camp several children came out to greet them. Patrick was known and respected by these people, but after exchanging greetings he bid them goodbye and they rode on.

It was close to darkness when they finally found a spot to camp in a hollow beside a small stream. Jamie looked after the horses while Kate and Patrick started a fire with buffalo chips and made supper. After they were finished they settled back, leaning onto their saddles, and talked while billions of brilliant stars filled the sky.

"Why didn't you want to camp with your Blackfoot friends?" Jamie asked.

"They don't have much food," Patrick replied. "If we were to camp with them they would feel obliged to provide a feast for us, and that might mean they would have nothing to eat tomorrow."

He stirred the fire for a moment, waiting for the coffee water to boil that was hung in a tin can over the flames, before he continued. "The Blackfoot are a proud people, led by Crowfoot, one of the great chiefs, but the buffalo are disappearing as the white hunters kill them off."

"How will they survive?" asked Kate.

"That's one of the reasons we must bring the herd of cattle back to Canada. Those animals will provide food for the Blackfoot as well as the police and everyone else. If we fail, soon everyone in the North-West Territories will be close to starvation."

"I didn't understand our mission was that important," Jamie said quietly into the gathering darkness.

The next morning they were up before dawn, ate a light breakfast of salt pork and hardtack biscuits, and were in the saddle as the sun broke the eastern horizon. In midmorning Kate spotted a pyramid of stones marking the international boundary. They were in the United States now — Montana Territory. There could be no protection by the North West Mounted Police south of the boundary line.

The further south they went the emptier the country seemed to become. The buffalo, that once had blackened the land, were gone. It was as if a great wind had swept them away and left the country empty of life.

By early afternoon they came across the rut marks of a wagon road. "It's the Whoop-Up Trail," Patrick announced, pleased with himself. "We're going to follow the whisky traders right down to Fort Benton."

"Why are we going there?" Kate asked.

"Provisions cost a lot less at Fort Benton than in Canada, and I need to talk to a banker there. It's the gathering place for this area. Steamboats come up the Missouri River as far as Fort Benton. Mountain men gather there along with traders. Blackfoot come down from their camps in the foothills to trade here. There are soldiers stationed at the fort, and there might even be some cattlemen. Who knows what sort of information we can pick up. "

Patrick was quiet for a moment and then he laughed. "But I've heard it said that it's the toughest place in the West, so we had better be careful."

Two days later they rode down into the deep valley, cut by the river, and found the town of Fort Benton, the first sizable centre any of them had seen in months. At first they passed a few log cabins on the outskirts of town set down in random order. Then the dusty street was lined with more prosperous wooden houses. Finally they came to Front Street that ran beside the river.

Along one side of Front Street was a complex of wharves and warehouses, called levies, where the big riverboats that came up the Missouri tied up and unloaded their cargo. On the other side of the street were hotels, saloons and merchants' establishments. On one corner stood the I.G. Baker Company, known as the greatest trading company in the Northwest. Down the street was the bank. Scores of horses were tied to hitching posts in front of the hotels and saloons.

As the three of them rode along the street they saw mountain men with long hair and beards lounging out in front of the saloons with women in fancy costumes. A prospector's pack train of five mules was being loaded beside a levy by a man dressed in buckskin. There were native people sitting on the boardwalks watching the scene along with well-dressed men in suits and broad-brimmed hats and women in long dresses. Everyone watched them as they rode along the street, as if they had deep suspicions of every newcomer who arrived among them.

"Now the two of you stick close to me," Patrick warned Kate and Jamie. "This place can be real trouble."

Patrick left them outside a hotel while he went in to inquire about rooms. As they waited Jamie glanced up and down the street. Suddenly he spotted two people he had hoped he would never see again: McCoy and Billy.

3

"They're here!" There was a touch of panic in Jamie's voice.

Kate studied the two from a distance. They were heading their way. "They can't do anything to us, Jamie."

"They want to get back at Patrick for arresting them."

Jamie would have found a way of ducking out of sight, but it was too late. McCoy swaggered down the boardwalk towards them, his hat tilted to the back of his head, his spurs jangling. He wore a gun slung low on his hip as if expecting trouble. Behind him Billy mimicked the same arrogant style.

McCoy greeted them with an insult. "Look who just got dragged into town. I wouldn't have expected you to leave that cozy little fort of the redcoats."

"Maybe they've come for a little excitement in a real town," added Billy as he slouched against a pillar in front of the hotel.

"We've come to get a herd of cattle," said Kate a little too defensively.

"Cattle is it?" McCoy seemed thoughtful for a moment. "Where's that friend of yours, McNeil?"

"He's inside the hotel now."

Jamie gave a hard look at his sister. He knew it was best to keep your business to yourself with people like this.

A slow sinister smile spread across McCoy's face. "Is that a fact now? Is that a fact? Cattle is it? I know a lot about cattle myself. Maybe I can help."

Patrick's voice cut across the conversation like a knife. "I need no help from the likes of you!" He had come out of the hotel and heard the last comment.

McCoy wheeled, his hand stroking his gun for an instant. "If it isn't the mounted policeman himself. Mister self-important."

"What are you doing here, McCoy?"

"That's what I should be askin' you. This is my town and my territory. You've got no authority here."

"I don't need any authority to deal with a man like you."

The two glared at each other before McCoy started to smile again. Jamie was beginning to recognize that he always smiled when he was angry or nervous.

"You're gonna find that things are a lot different down here in the United States of America. A lot different. For starters there ain't no law. It's every man for himself. So you'd best be lookin' over your shoulder all the time 'cause you never know who might be comin' up behind you."

With the warning delivered McCoy disengaged himself from the argument. A moment later he was continuing his stroll down the boardwalk with Billy close behind.

"They're trouble," Kate said more to herself than the others.

"We're not going to concern ourselves with people such as that," Patrick announced in his policeman-type voice.

"But is it true that there is no law here in Montana?" asked Jamie.

"Well, there are no policemen enforcing the law. That's true. But there are still laws. Anyway, come on now. We have lots to do while we are in town."

Patrick got them organized. Kate was to take their gear to their rooms in the hotel while Jamie looked after the horses. Patrick had to go to the bank. Afterwards, he told them, they would meet in the hotel lobby.

As he was about to go off Patrick suddenly remembered something. "Oh and Kate. Make sure you put your long skirt on. I want you to act like a proper lady while you are here."

Kate moaned a small protest, but she nodded. That was the one thing she had agreed to do on this trip.

Jamie led the three horses over to the livery stable. Once he had made arrangements to board them, he took off the saddles and gave the animals a good rubdown. He carefully examined every one of the horses' hooves to make sure that there were no sores or tender spots that had developed in the ride. Afterwards he gave each horse a feedbag of oats. They would need to be in good condition and well fed if they were to travel the long distances that lay ahead of them.

Kate was surprised to see how well furnished the lobby of the hotel was. There were leather settees and overstuffed chairs scattered about. Along one wall was a mahogany counter where guests checked in. Even the walls were lined in a rich deep-coloured wood panelling.

The furnishings of the hotel were much more luxurious than anything Kate had seen in Winnipeg and the Canadian West. Riverboats carrying goods up the Mississippi and Missouri were bringing fashion and comfort in their holds. The railroads had come as far as Bismarck in the Dakota Territory. Many predicted that once the railroad arrived in Montana the isolated life of the frontier would be over.

The two rooms Patrick had rented were not nearly as fancy as the lobby. A big brass bed was in one and two smaller beds in the other. Each room had a wooden wash stand with a flowered porcelain basin and towels. Water had to be carried in a big jug from the washroom down the hall.

Kate carefully washed her hair with cold water. It felt good to rinse off the dirt and dust of the trail. When she finished she put on her long skirt, the only one she owned, with a white blouse. She was brushing out her wet hair when Jamie arrived back from the livery stable.

"There are lots of people with money in this town," Jamie commented as he sunk onto the bed.

"Did you see the lobby? I bet it's as fancy as any in the East."

Jamie went down the hall to get some fresh water. When he came back he peeled off his shirt and began to wash.

Kate was thoughtful. "Do you think those men — Billy and that McCoy — are dangerous, Jamie?"

"If they did half the things they bragged about when I took them their food in jail, then they are pretty bad actors."

"Patrick thinks they are just riffraff."

"He still thinks like a policeman." Jamie paused for a moment, looking out the window towards the river. "McCoy is not one to play by the rules, and he hates Patrick. You can see it in his eyes."

When Jamie finished washing he changed into a clean shirt and the two of them went downstairs to wait for Patrick in the lobby. The hotel catered to people with money in the town of Fort Benton. Fancy-dressed women wandered in and out and men in business suits made their way through the lobby to meeting rooms in the back. Jamie and Kate felt more than a little out of place. When Patrick rejoined them they were relieved.

"Everything is set up," he told them, bubbling over with enthusiasm. "Things couldn't be better."

"Is the money in the bank?" Kate asked, knowing that had been one of Patrick's major concerns.

"Not only that but the banker that I met is going to give me a letter of introduction to Conrad Kohrs."

"Who's that?" asked Jamie.

"Kohrs is the largest rancher in the territory. He has a spread in Deer Lodge Valley in the mountains down south and west of here. He's a tough cattleman, but he has the reputation of being someone we can trust."

"It sounds like you are going to get your herd of cattle, Patrick." Jamie added.

Their leader smiled broadly. "I know we are going to make it work." He got to his feet and stretched. "So let's get organized. The banker will meet me here in the lobby in an hour or so with the letter. I'm going to wash up now. You go out and look around the town. We'll be ready to get on the trail again tomorrow morning."

Patrick climbed up the stairway of the fancy hotel whistling loudly, like a man who believed that he was about to make the deal of a lifetime. Jamie and Kate headed out onto the street, anxious to explore the frontier town.

It was late afternoon now, and Fort Benton was beginning to stir into life. Noise from one of the saloons they passed disturbed the calm. Glass shattered, there were angry voices, and then a man was pitched through the door into the street, propelled by the hard shove of two burly waiters.

The man, dressed like a prospector, gathered himself up from the dusty street. He cursed the saloon, and all its patrons, in a foul stream of words. It was obvious that he was drunk beyond comprehension. But in a moment he stopped his tirade, spoke a couple of words to himself and then tottered unsteadily towards another saloon.

A little farther along they came to a big wood frame structure with fancy glass windows with the name I.G. Baker Company, Merchant, in bold black letters. This was the most famous merchant in the West. Kate begged her brother to go inside, and the two of them pushed through the door setting off a bell to announce their arrival.

The place was filled with merchandise of all sorts, just as the sign had promised. There were big bolts of cloth for making clothing; stoves for cooking and heating; weapons from Winchesters to hand guns; all types of tools such as shovels, pitch forks and plows; hardware like nails, screws, bolts and tacks; and outfits for horses such as harnesses, saddles, blinkers and feedbags. In another part of the store food was sold in bulk: flour, sugar, rolled oats and even candy.

Kate stood in front of the counter admiring the variety of hard red and yellow and green candy that was on display. It had been so long since she had treats that she had almost forgotten that such a thing as candy existed.

"Yes, may I help you?" asked a store clerk wearing an apron, green eye-visor and elastic bands to hold up his shirt sleeves. He peered at them over his wire-framed eye glasses.

Kate was in such rapture at the sight of the candy that she was startled by the question. "No, I ... I'm just looking."

She turned around to find her brother staring over her shoulder at the candy. "Can we, Jamie?" she asked in a whisper.

"We don't have any money, Kate."

She turned back to look at the candy in a longing way, knowing it was completely beyond her reach. Slowly her brother steered her away from the counter towards the door.

"Would you like to have a sample?" the clerk suddenly asked.

Kate was so shocked that she looked first at her brother and then at the clerk. "You mean ..."

The clerk's smile softened his face. "Just a small sample so that when you are in town the next time you will know what you might like to buy."

The man offered a hard red candy to each of them, which they greedily popped into their mouths.

"Thank you. Thank you very much," they both said several times, overwhelmed at their good fortune. Slowly they backed out towards the door, thanking the clerk as they went.

With that small act of generosity the I.G. Baker Company had just won a lifetime of goodwill from the two of them.

As they were coming along the street back to the hotel, sucking happily on the hard candy, someone called out at them with a sarcastic edge to his voice. "There goes the pride of Canada." McCoy was leaning up against a hitching post. He looked drunk and unsteady. Beside him Billy scowled with a belligerence that spelled trouble. He lurched out towards them as they walked along the dusty street. Jamie turned to face him.

"Why'd you bring your little sister to this place?" Billy demanded, his words slurred as if he had been drinking. "Don't you know that this ain't no country for females?"

"I can look after myself," Kate replied defensively.

"You couldn't look after yourself in a Sunday school picnic." Billy laughed at his cleverness. "You need someone like me to protect you." And he lurched towards her.

Jamie stepped in front of his sister blocking his way. "You keep away from Kate," he said in a threatening voice. The two boys were about the same height and build.

Billy moved back a step as if to give himself room if there was a fight. "You're not man enough to look after her in this country. You're nothin' but a soft Canadian." He glanced back at McCoy as if playing the scene for that audience.

Jamie glared at him. Then he took his sister's arm and began to steer her down the street. "Let's get out of here, Kate, before Billy talks himself into trouble."

"You tryin' to insult me?"

"You're not smart enough to know an insult, Billy."

"Why'd you come down here anyway? The two of you plannin' to go work in the bars and saloons?"

Jamie swung around. He knew that was an insult directed at his sister.

Kate felt she had to intervene before something terrible happened. "We're going down to Kohrs' Ranch to get cattle to drive back to Canada."

"Kohrs' Ranch? You drivin' cattle? That's a laugh."

Billy's scorn had pushed Jamie beyond his limit now. "Stay away from us!"

"Yeah, and who's gonna make me?"

"I will! Now get out of my way!"

Suddenly Billy grabbed Kate by the wrist. She screamed. Jamie hit him hard in the chest with his shoulder with all of his strength. The boy dropped Kate's wrist and spilled over backwards onto the dusty street. Jamie was on top of him in a flash. The two boys rolled over and over in the dust, each trying to get a handhold on the other. Over the angry shouts and Kate's screams came McCoy's mocking laughter.

The boys were suddenly yanked apart and held at arm's length by Patrick McNeil. Both of them struggled against his iron grip. "What's this all about?" the former mounted police officer demanded.

"Let the two runts fight it out." McCoy shouted.

"McCoy, stay out of this or you will be in deep trouble!" Patrick demanded angrily.

"When are you gonna learn that you're nothin' down here, McNeil! Nothin'!"

Billy shook himself loose and went to rejoin McCoy. Patrick, holding Jamie sternly by the elbow, marched him back towards the hotel with Kate following. All the time they walked Patrick delivered a lecture.

"Jamie, I am disappointed in you. I thought you were smart enough to avoid a fight with the likes of someone like Billy. Maybe bringing you was a mistake. If there is any more trouble I am sending you right back to Canada! Understand?"

"But Billy picked the fight with Jamie," said Kate, trying to defend her brother.

"You have to avoid fights, especially with boys like that. Those bandits want to get at me for arresting them. The worst thing you can do is let them draw you into a fight. Then you are no better than them."

The town was beginning to settle for the night. Shops were closing up and business people were heading home for supper. Wagons wheeled down the road kicking up clouds of dust. Men were heading to the saloons while respectable people abandoned the streets.

Patrick had spoken his mind, and he left off the lecture. "Let's go and eat. Tomorrow we'll head out for Kohrs' Ranch. The sooner we get out of this town and leave McCoy and Billy behind the better."

The supper was surprisingly good. There was roast beef, potatoes and carrots. The big piece of apple pie that each of them had for dessert was delicious. By the time the meal was over everyone was in good spirits.

Later at night Jamie and Kate sunk into their beds. It had been a long time since either of them had slept in a wrought-iron bed with springs and a horse hair mattress. It was sheer luxury. But as they tried to get to sleep sounds from the street drifted up to them. There were angry voices, then shouts and curses. Shots — two, maybe three — broke the air, and then silence.

Jamie went to the window and looked out. Down the street a crowd milled around outside a saloon. The boy wondered if Billy and McCoy were somehow tied up with the latest round of trouble.

The next morning, as the dawn was breaking, Patrick pounded on their door and called for them to wake up. They got their gear together, went down the street to get a bite to eat and then went over to the big frame building of I.G. Baker Company. At precisely 8:00 a.m. the clerk, who had given them the candy the day before, unlocked the door.

Jamie was sent off to the livery stable to saddle up the horses while Patrick and Kate stayed to buy the provisions that they needed. The lovely warm spring day gave the boy's spirits a lift. It would be good to get out of town with its threats and dangers. He found the stable boy at the livery and paid him the fee for boarding the horses from the money Patrick had given him. He saddled the animals inside the stable and was leading them out through the big doors when he found Billy waiting for him. Jamie felt himself tense up in anticipation.

Billy appeared calm, but a slow anger simmered near the surface. "You gonna slink out of town without facing me again?"

"I've got nothing more to say to you, Billy." Jamie knew he had to avoid a fight at all costs. He kept walking, leading the horses with the reins in his hand.

Billy's voice was dark and threatening. "We're gonna meet again. I tell you that. Then you'll be sorry that our paths ever crossed. I promise you."

Jamie left Billy in the dusty street staring after him. The words of warning repeated ominously in his mind. What was Billy planning? They already knew too much about their business. Would they strike when they least expected it?

4

They loaded the new provisions into their saddlebags, mounted up, and the three of them rode out of town past the stores, hotels, saloons, houses and log cabins until once again they were out in open country. It was a relief to get away from Fort Benton and all its trouble.

A mile out of town the river had cut a huge cliff on the north shore, and the trail climbed steeply up onto the table-land. They rode in single file, with Patrick leading, Kate behind him, and Jamie bringing up the rear. The boy kept looking back over his shoulder, checking to see if anyone was following them. He was sure that he would spot Billy and McCoy, but there was no sign of them. Once they were at the top of the hill the boy began to relax. Maybe they were not being followed after all.

The trail headed west keeping to the tablelands along the north shore of the Missouri River. It was open country of rolling hills covered with rough grasslands that stretched as far as the eye could see. All day they rode hard, stopping barely long enough to rest their horses for a few minutes before they were in the saddle again.

In the afternoon Kate spotted mist rising up from the river. They left the trail and rode towards the sound of roaring water. At a cliff overlooking the river they could see a great waterfall surging over a ledge of rock. The Missouri was high from the spring runoff. As it tumbled over the cataract it made a deafening roar, sending mist high into the clear blue sky.

It was an impressive sight, but Patrick would not rest long to admire the view. Off they rode again, pushing their horses as hard as they could go. Towards nightfall they crested a hill. Patrick reined to a stop, and the others joined him on either side. To the west, far in the distance, a range of jagged snow-covered mountains rose up high above the rolling plain. Behind the mountains the setting sun cast yellow rays that glinted off the white snow and reflected reddish-golden colours on the clouds. Deep shadows sent a purple haze across the landscape.

"It's beautiful," said Jamie, awestruck.

Patrick smiled. "Wait until you see the foothills country of Canada. Where the prairie meets the mountains is a land as close to heaven as you will find anywhere on this globe."

They made camp beside a small stream. After something to eat they climbed into their bedrolls and were asleep in a matter of minutes. Before the break of dawn they were up again, had something to eat and were on the trail as the sun broke the eastern horizon.

Twice that day they had to ford sizable tributaries of the Missouri. Their horses waded into the water, and then when it got too deep, began swimming until they struck the gravel bottom on the other side. They were cold and wet, but still they pressed on.

That day they met two trappers coming back with their winter harvest of furs loaded onto pack animals. A party of prospectors passed them on the third day out. They had heard rumours of gold in the Rocky Mountain range, and they intended to find it. A little later Patrick spotted a party of native people in the distance.

"They are from the Blood tribe," he explained. "The Blood are part of the Blackfoot confederacy."

"Will they give us trouble?" Kate asked.

"The mounted police have been good to the Blood. If you ever meet them make sure that they know that you are a Canadian."

The river had turned south, and on the third day out they found themselves in a country of high rolling mountains and bluffs. The trail tried to keep to the easiest grade, but often it went up or down treacherously steep hills. They rode through pine forests and had to cross fast-running creeks. The horses and riders were getting tired, but Patrick would not let them rest until sundown.

The next morning they came into the gold mining town of Helena but barely paused long enough to get directions. Picking up a new trail heading west, they climbed a long way up towards the MacDonald Pass. Stage coaches used this road, but it was still a difficult climb up.

"This is the Continental Divide," Patrick explained as they got towards the summit of the pass. "All the water east of the divide flows down into the Atlantic Ocean. West of the divide it flows towards the Pacific."

Kate was impressed. "I didn't know that we were that far away from home."

The trip over the mountains was exhausting. When they finally got through the pass they camped by the Little Blackfoot River. The next morning all three of them took a bath in the cold waters of the river and then rode into Deer Lodge Valley. By noon they had found the headquarters of Conrad Kohrs' ranch.

It was a big spread with a half-dozen corrals holding horses and cattle and a scattering of sheds and stables. The house was a two-storey, white, wooden structure with chimneys at either end, a porch on the front and surrounded by a white picket fence.

Kate was impressed with the sheer size of the house and the operation. "I haven't seen a house that big since we left Ontario."

"The house looks like one of those church buildings in Manitoba," added Jamie.

They followed the fence to a long group of buildings that were the bunkhouses for the cowboys and hired hands. Patrick reined in, and the three of them dismounted. As they were looking around a tall, stocky, bearded man of about thirty-five with fair hair and a full beard came out of the ranch house. He was dressed in a long morning coat with matching trousers and black Stetson hat.

"We're looking for Conrad Kohrs," Patrick inquired. "Could you tell us where we could find him?"

"You're looking at him. And who might you be?" Kohrs spoke with a German accent.

Patrick smiled broadly and held out his hand. "Sir, I'm pleased to meet you. I'm Patrick McNeil, recently retired from the North West Mounted Police, and I've come all the way from Canada to buy a herd of cattle." The two men shook hands warmly.

"Canadian. I bought this spread from Johnny Grant, a Canadian Métis. If it's cattle that you want then you've come to the right place, Mister McNeil."

Jamie tied up the horses and came to stand beside his sister. They listened quietly as the two men talked.

"I want to drive the herd up to the foothills in Canada," Patrick explained. He spoke in a formal manner, like a subordinate talking to an officer.

"I've heard it said that the grazing land is rich in that country. If it is anything like Deer Lodge Valley, you will do well."

"The grass is better, sir. Infinitely better. With chinook winds the winter feed is good and the animals prosper."

"Is that a fact or a hope?"

"I believe it to be a fact, sir."

Kohrs smiled. "I'm a simple German immigrant, Mr. McNeil, but I've learned that in this country you have to work

on the basis of facts. Hopes are useless." His speech suggested that there was nothing simple about this man.

It was only then that the attention of the cattle baron
shifted to the two young people standing by their horses. His
face lit up at the sight of Kate. "What's a young girl doing so
far away from the comforts of civilization?"

"I'm Kate Bains, and I can look after myself as well as
any of these men," she said with some forcefulness.

Kohrs smiled at Kate's reply. "I like your spirit," and he
laughed. "My wife, Augusta, will appreciate you, and that is
a fact. Come, I want you to meet her."

Kohrs took Kate by the elbow and, ignoring Patrick,
steered her towards the back door of the ranch house. The
others followed behind. Once inside he began calling,
"Augusta! Augusta! Come and see who's arrived!" Then he
turned to explain to Kate. "She is always complaining that
there are no females willing to come out to live in this wild
country."

They had entered the big sitting room at the front of the
house. A young woman of about twenty-five set aside her
needlepoint and rose from a chair to greet them. She was
imposing, almost six feet tall, but she had soft, intelligent
eyes. Her dark hair was swept up into a bun at the back of her
head, and she wore a beautiful blue embroidered dress that
flowed to the floor. She had the graces of an aristocratic
European lady.

"My dear," she said, holding out her hand to Kate. "What
is a young girl like you doing out on the rough frontier all
alone?"

"I'm with my brother, Jamie, and Patrick. We're here to
buy cattle," she explained. The others had come into the room
and stood shyly watching the females.

"Oh, I see, I see. But look at you now." Augusta stood
back and examined Kate.

For the first time Kate felt self-conscious to be in her breeches. "I just use these for riding," she tried to explain shyly.

"It's perfect for this wild country. The best of fashion." She beamed. "You are something special. But what's your name, my dear?"

"Kate ... Kate Bains."

"Well you are a welcome addition to Kohrs' Ranch, Miss Kate Bains. Please, will you join me?"

Kate understood something of the loneliness that women on the frontier had to endure. Even women of wealth and prestige lived for months and years without having another female they felt comfortable to talk to. Augusta settled Kate on the sofa beside her and then gave directions to her husband.

"Now you just go off and talk about your business, Conrad. Kate and I are going to have a nice chat."

Kohrs was more than pleased with developments, and it put him in a good frame of mind to talk about cattle. He led Patrick and Jamie out onto the porch in front of the house, and they settled in chairs overlooking the broad expanse of valley. In the distance high hills rose up towards white-capped mountains. Cattle could be seen as mere dots grazing on hillsides. The late afternoon sun warmed them as they sat talking. Quiet settled on the land broken only by the low bellows from the cattle held in the corrals.

Patrick explained his plans in a crisp businesslike manner. "We would like to buy 500 head of cattle to drive north into Canada, Mr. Kohrs. The market is growing in our country with the arrival of the police and other whites. Now that the buffalo is disappearing the Blackfoot tribe will need beef to survive."

"I've heard it said that the mounted police brought peace to that country." Like his wife their host had a formal air about him.

"I was part of that force."

"That's what we need in Montana: a good police force." Kohrs looked off across the valley. "Cattle rustlers and thieves operate out in the open and there is no one to enforce the law. The bandits are taking over the territory."

"We've met some of them."

"Men here have been known to take the law into their own hands in this country."

"Not in Canada. The North West Mounted Police always get their man."

They sat and chatted about the affairs of each of their countries for some time, getting to know each other, so that they would feel comfortable doing business together. Kohrs explained that he sold cattle in the mining communities and every fall they drove cattle to the railheads in Wyoming and Bismarck, Dakota. Finally the rancher steered the conversation back towards the issue at hand.

"So you want to buy some cattle, Mr. McNeil."

Things were going very well. Patrick had just one more hurdle to cross before they could talk price. "I just have one problem, sir. I hope I can speak plainly. I am going to need help to buy this herd. I have gathered money from my friends in the police force, and I have my own money, but I don't believe it will be enough to buy the herd."

The rancher stiffened. "Are you asking me for credit?"

"Just for a short time, sir. I have enough to buy provisions and make a down payment. As soon as we get the herd to Canada I will sell the steers. That will give me enough money to pay the wages of the cowboys and settle the debt."

"You are asking me to bankroll this enterprise. I am not in the banking business, Mr. McNeil."

"But it will only be for a short time, sir."

Kohrs got to his feet. "I need money to run my own operation. If I was to give credit all sorts of people would be opening up in competition to me."

"I am going to take the herd to Canada. There is no way that I will be in competition with you." Patrick and Jamie got to their feet to join their host.

"How long will it be before you can repay me?"

"Five months. Six months at the outside." The mood had cooled.

Kohrs stared across the valley for the longest time before speaking. "Well let me think on it, Mr. McNeil. We will talk about it again." He moved towards the door, indicating the conversation was over. "I would like all of you to come to dinner tonight. It is always a pleasure to meet visitors to this isolated part of the country. Of course you are welcome to stay in the bunkhouse."

The rancher led them into the big house where they found Kate and Augusta talking and laughing. Despite the difference in their ages they had already found much to talk about.

"Conrad, the adventures of this young girl are remarkable. What an age we live in where women are accepted almost the equal of men."

"We are the equal to men," Kate said proudly. She had been raised by her mother to feel on a par with any of her brothers.

Kohrs smiled. "I wouldn't say that, young lady."

They shook hands all around. The time was set for dinner and Kate, Jamie and Patrick took their leave.

As soon as they were out of the house Patrick explained his fears. "He's not going to give me the loan."

"What loan?" Kate asked.

"Kohrs has to give me credit or I won't be able to buy the cattle. I don't think he is going to do it."

Jamie was annoyed. "You didn't tell us that you would need a loan to buy the herd, Patrick."

"I thought it would be no problem."

"You mean we have come all of this way without knowing whether he would give credit?" The boy was beginning to wonder about Patrick's ability as a businessman.

"I thought he would."

"Maybe he was just bluffing," suggested Kate optimistically, but Jamie was concerned about this unexpected development.

They led their horses over to the stable. Jamie took off the saddles and began to groom the animals while the others gathered their gear. They were heading over to the bunkhouse when Augusta appeared in the doorway. She was an impressive sight in her full gown.

"Kate, dear, I want you to come and stay at the house."

"I don't mind the bunkhouse."

"I know you can look after yourself, but I don't want you staying with all of those rough cowboys. It's not proper."

"You go ahead, Kate," urged her brother.

"I insist. Now come along right now. I'm going to get someone to pour you a hot bath."

How could Kate refuse that type of offer? Once inside Augusta called to the cook and soon hot water was being heated on the stove for a bath. In no time Kate was luxuriating in steaming water in the fancy cast-iron bathtub.

The long, hard ride had taken its toll on her. The warmth of the water eased her aching muscles and bones. She soaked until the water was cold. Only then did she climb out and towel herself off. Afterwards she put on her long skirt and blouse and went downstairs.

Augusta smiled as she came into the sitting room. "That's a little more feminine than those riding pants that you wear."

"I like the pants. It makes the men forget that I am a girl."

"Don't you like being a girl, Kate?"

"I do, but if men treat you in a special way it means that they think that you're not as good as they are."

Augusta was nodding. "Women work a good deal harder than most men, especially out here in the West. They have children to look after and a household to run, but still the men think it's their world."

They chatted until dinner time. Patrick and Jamie arrived, dressed in their best clothes. Both of them looked nervous. It was intimidating to be invited to dine in the house of someone as wealthy and powerful as Conrad Kohrs, and Patrick had his business venture to worry about.

When they all had gathered they went into the dining room and ate a wonderful four-course meal. After dinner the men, Jamie included, retired to the smoking room across the hall while the two ladies went to the sitting room. Conrad offered Patrick a cheroot, poured him a drink of sherry, and the two men smoked and drank while Kohrs delivered the bad news.

"I am sorry, Mr. McNeil. I have given your proposal some thought, but I have decided that I cannot give you credit."

Patrick reasoned with him, then argued strongly that it was in everyone's interest if the loan was made. He reminded him that even the bank manager in Fort Benton had given him a letter of recommendation, but it did no good. In the end Patrick was reduced to pleading, but Kohrs had made up his mind. He would not give the loan.

After their cigars the men rejoined the ladies, but the conversation was strained. Patrick remained quiet and withdrawn. Kate was to sleep in the house that night, and when it came time to draw the evening to a close Jamie found that he was the one offering thanks to the Kohrs on behalf of Patrick and himself.

On the way back to the bunkhouse Patrick expressed his total defeat. "It's over, Jamie. All I can do is go back to Canada and give the money back to the people who believed in me."

"But you've got a little money. You could buy a few cattle to make the trip worthwhile."

"Probably no more than twenty-five head. We've got to have about 500 to make it worth the effort. I was counting on credit from Kohrs. Now I'm finished. What am I going to do?"

Jamie didn't know what to say. He could have criticized Patrick for coming all that way without working out the details, but that would be useless. One of the things he liked about him was his buoyant optimism, although that was what got him into trouble.

The boy tried to think things through carefully. Kohrs would not give Patrick credit because he did not believe he would be successful, or did not trust him. Somehow it did not seem fair. They had been sitting despondently on the edge of their beds in the bunkhouse considering their options when Jamie got to his feet and headed out the door.

"Where are you going?" Patrick asked.

"To see Kate," was his only reply, and then he disappeared into the darkness.

Jamie was in luck. When he pounded on the kitchen door the cook answered and agreed to fetch Kate for him. His sister came into the kitchen a moment later, and the two whispered together.

"What's wrong?" she asked.

Jamie explained the situation as carefully as he could. "Without credit Patrick cannot buy the cattle and he has nothing," the boy explained.

"That's terrible," Kate was now as upset as her brother. "What can we do?"

"I was thinking that if you could talk to Augusta ..." but just at that moment Augusta came into the kitchen.

She smiled to see Jamie and Kate, but just as quickly her expression changed when she saw the deep worry on their faces. "What is it?" she asked.

Jamie felt trapped. It was best to have Kate deal with the difficult issue, but now that he had been asked he felt he had to tell the truth. "It's ... it's just that ..."

"Just tell me."

But it was Kate who explained. "Patrick asked your husband for credit to buy cattle and he refused."

"Refused?"

"Yes, he ..."

Augusta looked stunned. "You don't need to draw a map for me. Conrad Kohrs may think he is the head of the household, but he has another thing coming if he believes I will stand for this! Leave it to me. I will speak to him."

At that Augusta marched out of the kitchen calling her husband's name in a loud commanding voice. "Conrad ... Conrad ... I must have a word with you right now!"

Kate and Jamie looked at each other for a moment. Then the boy eased out of the back door and into the night. It was best to be absent when two powerful characters like Augusta and Conrad Kohrs had a disagreement.

5

The next morning, after a good meal in the cookhouse, Jamie and Patrick were tending to their horses when Conrad Kohrs approached.

"I must say that you have powerful friends, Patrick." The rancher seemed gruff and unfriendly. "I will grant you the credit to buy 500 head of cattle."

"You will, sir?" Patrick was flabbergasted at the news.

"But I want payment in full in six months. Plus interest. I am a businessman after all, though I'm starting to doubt my own judgment."

Patrick could hardly believe the good news. "You mean … you will give me the full credit to buy the herd?"

"You heard me."

"I have some money, Mr. Kohrs."

"We'll work out the details. I'll get the papers drawn up, but first you'll have to head up into the high country to pick your animals. I'll get someone to take you there. By the time you're back you can sign up and be on your way."

"Thank you, sir. Thank you very much. I don't know what to say."

"It's not me that you have to thank. Just pay me in six months, and I'll be happy. I don't operate a charity, you know."

With that Conrad Kohrs walked brusquely past them to talk to a group of cowboys who were over by the icehouse.

"Why is he so unfriendly?" Patrick whispered to Jamie.

"Augusta made him change his mind."

"Augusta? But why?"

Jamie could hardly believe it. "You are slow, Patrick. Kate and Augusta became friends. When Kate told her that Conrad wouldn't give you credit Augusta went to him and told him he had to change his mind. That's why he's annoyed."

Patrick looked dumbfounded. "So ... so it was Kate who got the loan for me."

"Maybe the next time you say something about girls you might remember this."

"You Patrick McNeil?" A tall, rangy cowboy, who had been standing with the others, had come up to them quietly.

"Yes."

"Chisholm's the name. The ranch boss says I'm to take you up to the high country." The cowboy spoke slowly with a southern accent. He wore dungarees with a big leather belt, cowboy boots and a plaid shirt. His broad-brimmed hat was high in the crown, Texan style.

"Where's that?" Patrick asked.

"She's half a day's ride. We'd best be goin' soon."

They had most of their gear together. Patrick saddled the horses while Jamie went up to the big ranch house to tell Kate. He found her sitting with Augusta around the dinner table just finishing breakfast.

"They're taking us up into the high country to get the cattle, Kate."

His sister smiled and then glanced at Augusta. "I heard that might be a possibility."

The boy shifted awkwardly on his feet. "We need to thank you, Mrs. Kohrs."

"It's Conrad that you have to thank. He's the one who made the final decision."

Jamie nodded. "We did thank him, but ..." He did not need to finish. They all knew who persuaded Conrad Kohrs to change his mind.

Augusta continued with a little advice. "Just remember to pay him back and on time. If you do that you have made a friend for the rest of your life."

"Are we leaving now, Jamie?" Kate asked.

"Patrick's getting our gear together. We're almost ready to ride out."

"I'll just be a minute." Kate leaped up and rushed for the staircase, almost tripping over her long skirt.

"You don't have to go, Kate, dear," said Augusta. "You can stay here with me and join the others when they drive the cattle through."

Kate paused, her hand on the rail of the staircase. Augusta had come to feel like an older sister to her. The two of them had talked for hours, and Kate had learned just how lonely the older woman had become since she had arrived at that isolated ranch. Money and power could not buy friendship and happiness.

"Augusta, I've got to go," she tried to explain. "I'm sorry. I started with Jamie and Patrick, and I have to do my part until the cattle arrive in Canada. Do you understand?"

Augusta swept to her feet with regal grace. "I do understand, Kate. Nothing will stop you. I admire that." But there was sadness in her eyes.

Kate rushed to give her a hug. They shared the experience of living in a man's world out on the very edge of the frontier, and it had bonded them into friendship.

Augusta hugged her friend hard and then whispered. "Go. Go Kate. They are waiting for you."

The young girl broke free from the embrace and raced up the stairway, shouting to her brother. "Wait for me, Jamie! I just have to get my things!"

Minutes later they were up on their horses, heading for the trail to the high country. Kate was wearing her riding gear of breeches, shirt and a jacket. Her skirt and blouses were packed away.

There were five riders that set out for the high country. The three from Canada were led by Chisholm, the slow talking man from Texas. The other was a black man by the name of Josh who also spoke with a broad southern accent.

Josh was a quiet man with careful watchful eyes. He was tall, well over six feet, with broad shoulders and strong arms. Kate rode with him for a while and learned that he had been born a slave in the state of Alabama. He had been a cowboy for over ten years now and liked to ride in the northern states because he was treated better than in the South.

All morning long they were in the saddle, climbing into the Flint Creek Range of mountains that lay to the west of them. Some parts of the slopes were covered with pine trees but most were open grasslands. When they turned back to look where they had come from the winding valley stretched out at their feet. To the east was the Continental Divide mountain range. Everywhere they saw signs of cattle and horses, but there were no fences to pen them in.

After an hour's ride up into the mountains Kate began to feel a little cold and had to put on her warm winter jacket. Then it started to rain. Chisholm and Josh took out their oilskin slickers that they had tied onto the back of the saddles and put them on, but the others had to endure the downpour. Soon they were soaked to the skin. The rain came down so heavily that water ran down the hill in rivulets. The trail, beaten into dust by thousands of cattle, turned into a mud track.

"Why do we have to go to the high country?" Jamie asked Chisholm, when he had the chance.

"Roundup's almost finished, and the cattle have been moved up into the summer pastures in the mountains," he explained. "In winter they are kept down in the valleys 'cause the snow's not as deep and the grass is better."

That was as much as they could get out of Chisholm. Short and to the point seemed to be the way the Texan dealt with everything. He concentrated on the trail, picking out the best footing for the horses and letting the others follow behind as best as they could.

Finally, after they had been on the trail for about five hours, they broke over a ridge and found the Kohrs' Ranch summer camp nestled in a hollow of hills to give some protection from the incessant wind. There was a corral filled with horses and a chuck wagon for feeding the men had been set up. These were the only structures in the isolated camp. Several of the cowboys had rigged up canvas lean-tos near the chuck wagon, to give them a little shelter. A big bonfire was flaming, and around it a group of cowboys were drinking coffee.

When they rode in one of the men at the fire came over to greet them. "This here's Curly," Chisholm said by way of introduction. "He's the camp boss."

Patrick swung off his horse and extended his hand to Curly. "Patrick McNeil. It's good to meet you. I've made a deal with Mr. Kohrs to purchase 500 head of cattle. We're going to drive them north into Canada."

Curly stood with his hands on his hips. "North? Will you be goin' up through Blackfoot country?"

Patrick smiled. "That's the only way to get to Canada."

"Them Blackfoot sure have been givin' us cattlemen trouble. They seem to think that this is their land."

"I was with the North West Mounted Police in Canada. They like us."

"Is that a fact." But Curly did not look convinced.

The two men went off to discuss cattle, and Josh and Chisholm went over to the fire to talk to friends. It had stopped raining, but it had left Jamie and Kate cold and damp. They tied up their horses and went over to the fire to get some of the warmth from the flames.

There was still a little work to finish the roundup. Every spring the cowboys combed the hills and valleys searching for the cattle owned by the ranch. There were no fences in that country, and the cattle ranged for miles. Once they were rounded up the herd was counted, checked for disease and then driven into the high country for the summer. In the spring roundup there was a new crop of calves that had to be branded with the Kohrs' mark.

Kate and Jamie were standing by the fire when a young cowboy, mounted on a brown gelding, chased a yearling calf towards the fire. The horse stayed on the calf's tail. The cowboy circled his rope over his head and then deftly let it go. The noose dropped over the calf's head. At that very moment the cowboy tied his end of the rope around the horn of his saddle and reined his horse to hard stop. The rope went taut, stopping the calf in midstride. At the same instant the cowboy was out of the saddle. He grabbed the calf and threw him to the ground and held him there. By then a cowboy tending the fire was there with the red-hot branding iron. He held it to the calf's left hind quarter until the mark of the Kohrs' Ranch was burned into its flesh. The calf bellowed in pain. Then the cowboy loosened the rope from around its neck, and it was let go to run back to its mother. The whole thing had taken little more than a minute to complete.

Jamie was amazed at the speed and sheer skill of the cowboy. "I thought I was good at handling a horse, but I've never seen anything like that."

"The horse and rider worked like a team," added Kate.

"Do you think I can ever do that?"

"If you're going to be a cowboy you're going to have to learn."

In time Patrick came over to the fire and explained to Jamie and Kate what was going to happen.

"We're getting 500 head of cattle. Two hundred and fifty of them will be steers that we will sell as soon as we get back to Canada. With that money we can pay off the debt to Kohrs. The rest will be cows and calves. They'll be the base of the herd that we are going to build."

"What about cowboys for the drive?" Jamie asked.

"Curly tells me that with 500 head, we will only need six men. They have finished their roundup and have let a number of cowboys go. We'll be able to hire a crew without any trouble. We'll also need a cook. Kate will be cook's help and Jamie will work as the wrangler looking after the horses."

"I don't want to help the cook!" said Kate, feeling insulted. "I want to help Jamie. Why can't I be a cowboy?"

"Kate, you don't have the skills to be a cowboy. I'm not even sure that Jamie can handle the job of the wrangler."

"What do you mean?" The boy was annoyed. "I can handle horses."

"It'll be your job to look after thirty or more horses. You'll have to know how to cut them out, rope them and make sure that they can be ridden. It's a big job."

"I can do it," said Jamie stubbornly. "You just watch. I can do anything with a horse."

"I hope so because it's a long ride back to the Canadian foothills country."

Not long after they were given instructions about their jobs Patrick rode out of the camp with Curly to look at cattle. Kate and Jamie were still burning from what he had told them.

"I'm not going to be a cook's help," stormed Kate. "I didn't come all of this way to wash dishes and scrub pots."

But her brother was hardly listening to her. He kept thinking about how the cowboy had used his horse to ride down the calf, then roped him, ready for branding. He knew that he could not do that now. And how was he going to look after those half-wild western ponies? He would have to look after them, rope them, train them and keep them in good shape. How was he going to manage?

"Word is that you're gonna be the wrangler on the cattle drive, boy." Jamie had not seen Chisholm approach him.

"That's right." He stood up to his full height to impress but was still shorter than the Texan.

"I don't even see a lariat on your saddle. A wrangler has to be like a piano player with his rope."

"I can handle it. You'll see."

"Ever looked after horses?"

"All the time."

"How about ridin' a western horse? We've got one in the corral. He's right gentle. A stallion. Why don't you give him a ride, wrangler?"

"Yeah, all right. Sure."

The Texan turned to the others with a smile on his face. "Go and rope the black stallion, there Josh. We got ourselves a rider."

A moment later Jamie found himself in the corral. Josh had tied a big, strong stallion to a post while it was being saddled. The horse pulled against its tether, whipping its head back and forth as it tried to get free. Whenever anyone came close he kicked its back hooves. This would be no gentle ride. This was a wild stallion — what cowboys called a bronco.

They were going to have fun at his expense, but Jamie knew there was no backing down now. It was better to be thrown from the horse than to be seen as afraid to try to ride it. The cowboys saddled the stallion and then backed away. The whole outfit, now, had climbed up onto the top rail of the corral and were yelling and shouting. Kate joined them with fear in her stomach. Everyone was set to enjoy the show of a greenhorn getting thrown off a bronco.

Jamie approached the stallion cautiously. It looked at him with eyes bugging out in terror. The boy began to talk calmly, in a soothing voice. "Easy now. Nothing to be frightened of. Easy now …"

He knew the sound of his voice eased the fear of the horse. He talked for some time and then put his hand on the animal's neck and moved close so that the horse could get his scent.

The cowboys were shouting impatiently now. "Come on!" "Get up and ride him, boy!" "Are you afraid?"

But Jamie ignored them. Long ago he had been taught that you took your time with horses or paid the price. Slowly he patted the stallion's neck and talked into its ear. Gradually the terror went out of the animal, and it calmed. Then, in a deliberate way, the boy reached up and undid the reins that were tied to the post. The horse pulled away. Jamie held on to the reins firmly. He knew he had to show the animal who was in control. A tremor went through its body. Slowly Jamie eased along the left flank and put his foot into the stirrup. In an easy fluid motion, so as not to startle the horse, he swung his leg over and settled into the saddle.

Suddenly the horse erupted. It seemed to leap straight up into the air and land on all four feet with a hard, bone-crushing jar. Then it kicked with its back legs so violently that its back reared up. It was all that Jamie could do to hold on for dear life. His legs clutched onto the horse's sides. One hand held onto the pommel of the saddle and the other pulled hard on the reins.

Teach it that you're in control, was what went through the boy's head. Hold on. Don't let it throw you. But the stallion was off across the corral bucking and kicking and throwing its body in every way possible in an attempt to get rid of this burden that stuck like a burr to its back.

Jamie clutched the horse's flanks with every ounce of strength in his legs. The bronco bucked and reared, coming down with jarring effect, but still the boy held on. The cowboys were yelling and shouting like wild men, but Jamie could not hear a thing. He would ride this stallion if it took every ounce of strength that he had.

The horse had bucked across the corral, turned and bucked again. It came down with a crushing jar. The boy lost his grip with his legs. The stallion was in the air again, kicking hard. Jamie flew out of the saddle and landed on the ground with such force that it shook him to the core.

6

The boy was dusting himself off when his sister came running across the corral to him. "Jamie! Jamie! are you all right?"

He was watching the stallion at the other end of the corral continuing to buck and leap about as it tried to get rid of the saddle. A cowboy climbed off the fence and threw his lariat around its neck and tied it to the post.

"Are you sure that you're not hurt?"

Jamie said nothing. He felt annoyed at himself. What would the cowboys think of him now that he had been thrown in his first try at riding a bronco?

"You done good, boy." Chisholm had come up along with the other cowboys.

"That's one mean stallion," added Josh. "Not many cowboys would o'stayed aboard that long."

Jamie grinned. Coming from old hands those were compliments. Impulsively, perhaps foolishly, he said. "I'm going to ride him again."

"You can't do that, Jamie!" Kate was alarmed. She knew the stubborn quality of her brother only too well.

"I can break him this time."

"All right, boy," said Josh. "Teach that horse who's the boss."

Jamie felt a new sense of confidence and strength. Again he talked to the stallion and stroked it softly on the neck. By the time he took off the rope the horse had calmed. Jamie moved along its flank. The animal shied away from him, baring its teeth and whinnying.

Slowly Jamie put his foot in the stirrup, threw his leg over the horse's back and eased into the saddle. The stallion tossed its neck. Jamie yanked the reins so it could feel the bit in its mouth. Suddenly the horse bucked hard and then bucked again. Jamie clamped his legs around its flanks. He was determined that he would not be thrown.

The horse raced across the corral. When it got to the split-rail fence it stopped dead. It took all of Jamie's strength to hold onto the saddle, but this time he stuck like glue. He pulled hard on the reins to the right, and the horse responded. Jamie kicked it gently on the ribs. The stallion reared up on his back legs and then began to run. Three times the horse raced around the corral before Jamie was able to bring it to a halt.

The stallion was covered in lather and breathing hard. Slowly Jamie dismounted and stood beside it, stroking its neck and talking quietly to ease its fears. The boy knew that the animal would need a lot more training, but this was a good beginning.

Chisholm went out of his way to give him praise. "You did well, boy. You might just be a wrangler yet."

Jamie had finished rubbing down the stallion when Josh showed up with a grass lariat and a new pair of gloves. "Looks like you want to be a cowboy," the big black man said with his southern accent. "So you got to learn to use the rope."

Josh was a great teacher. He held the lariat in his hand and began to work with it. "You've got to spin that rope hard to open the loop. Put some muscle into it, boy." He threw it and the loop dropped over a fence post as easy as pie.

Jamie tried and then Kate. Over and over again they threw the rope until they started to get the hang of it.

"That's good," Josh said with his big smile. "Now you've got to learn to ride a horse full out, put a lariat over a steer's head and drop him dead in his tracks. When you can do that you've got the makin's of a cowboy."

Jamie and Kate were still practising with the rope when Patrick returned. "It looks good, very good," he told them. "These cattle are in excellent shape. If we drive them slow and easy they'll be nice and fat when we get them to Canada, and they'll bring a good price."

Kate had been waiting for this opportunity to talk to the trail boss. "Patrick, I don't want to work with the cook. I want to help Jamie as the wrangler."

"You said that you were willing to work. Girls do cooking and things like that."

"I can ride just as well as Jamie, and we're both learning how to rope."

"You work with the cook, and I don't want to hear another word of complaint. Now I've got to go and talk with Curly. Jamie, you're going to have to get the horses together. Better talk to someone about that."

Kate went off to sit by herself. She was convinced that no one understood her or even cared about her. Maybe she should have stayed with Augusta. Or maybe she shouldn't have come on this trip at all. Patrick seemed to think that she was more of a nuisance than a help.

Jamie saw Kate sitting off by herself. She was too strong-minded for her own good, he sometimes thought, but he knew his younger sister had her strengths. He went to sit beside her.

"Don't be upset, Kate," he said, trying to sympathize with her.

She turned on him. "Don't you feel sorry for me, Jamie Bains. You're just like Patrick and the others."

"I didn't say anything."

"You don't have to! You get to be the wrangler and look after the horses, and I have to help the cook. It's just not fair."

Jamie knew there was some truth in what she said. He was excited about being the wrangler. If he had been the cook's help he would have hated it. He thought about that for a moment and then said to her, "Kate, you can help me with the horses. I've got a lot to do and I don't know if I can do everything."

She looked at her brother. He sounded as if he was asking for help. "Well, if I help you with the horses maybe you can help me with the cook."

"Yeah. Sure I will. We'll share the chores."

Kate smiled at her brother. He really did understand what she was feeling.

The next morning over breakfast around the fire Curly organized his crew to bring the cattle down from the hills. Patrick took the opportunity to talk to the rest of the men.

"I'm looking for a crew to drive this herd up to Canada. I'll need six drovers and a cook."

One of the cowboys spoke up. "You sure that's safe? You'll be goin' through Blackfoot country."

Patrick always felt confident dealing with this problem. "I know the Blackfoot. I was a member of the North West Mounted Police in Canada, and the Blackfoot respect anyone who has anything to do with the force."

"I dunno. A man could lose his scalp pretty easy."

"They're our friends. We'll have no problem. I can guarantee it. Now I know some men have been let go by Mr. Kohrs because the roundup is finished. I can promise top wages. Come and see me."

But the warning about the Blackfoot made the men wary. After breakfast Curly's permanent crew scattered to round up the cattle and drive them down to the pasture. The other men hung around the camp considering the offer made by Patrick. Chisholm and Josh approached Jamie to talk about it.

"You know this Patrick McNeil, do you, boy?" Chisholm asked.

Jamie nodded.

"Is he a good man?"

"Absolutely." Jamie felt he should be positive.

"Can he deliver what he promises?" asked Josh.

"He's been good to us," volunteered Kate.

"I drove cattle up the Chisholm Trail four seasons in a row," said Chisholm in his Texas drawl. "That's how I got my name. Josh here is an experienced man. If we come with your Mister Patrick we want cash on the barrel head when we deliver the cattle. You understand?"

"You have to talk to Patrick about that. I can't guarantee about the money." The boy felt uneasy about this part of the arrangements. Patrick had already delivered one surprise.

Chisholm was thoughtful. "I like you, boy, and the girl here, but I don't know about your Mister Patrick, and I'm not sweet on the idea of goin' through Blackfoot land."

Most of the day the cowboys who had been let go by Kohrs' Ranch talked about the possibility of being drovers. They discussed it together and then talked with Patrick. They dickered over their wages and what position each of them would have. Two of the men were nervous about the Blackfoot and refused to go. Another man wanted to head over the mountains to look at Idaho and Oregon. In the end six men agreed to sign on.

Chisholm and Josh were the first to sign. They were experienced drovers and liked the rhythm of the work. The other four had never been on a long drive before, but they were cowboys who knew the skills of their trade.

Mike was a high-spirited Irishman who spoke with a broad accent and a sharp tongue. He looked every inch a cowboy except that he insisted on wearing a bowler hat rather than the broad-brimmed variety favoured by most cowboys.

"I brought this hat across a whole ocean," he once told Kate. "And 'tis sure that I'm not going to part with it now."

There were two farm boys who had been cowboys from the time that they had left home. Fergie was from Kansas, where his parents tried to scrape a homestead out of land that turned dry as desert as soon as the crops grew up. The other was a twenty-five-year-old called Buck, because he had been thrown from so many horses. Buck liked to talk, but he never mentioned his family.

Strangest of all was a man the others called Trapper. He was part Indian from the Navaho tribe. No one knew how or why he came to the northern range, so far away from his family, but the rumour was that he was running away from something. Trapper didn't talk much, and he seemed to have a grudge against cattle, but he was the best horseman that they had.

This was the crew of drovers. Every man signed a piece of paper stating his wages of $40 a month plus meals. Some, like Mike, signed in an elaborate hand, while Trapper, Fergie and Buck simply marked their X on the paper. They could neither read or write.

It was on the evening of the third day in the high country that a cowboy rode up from the ranch headquarters bringing food and gear on pack horses. Over supper he casually mentioned to Jamie that he had met a couple of friends of theirs.

The boy was puzzled. "Friends? We don't have any friends around here."

"They were askin' for you at the bunkhouse. One was a hard-lookin' critter ridin' a hungry pony, and the other was a boy about your age."

Jamie was panicked. He turned to Kate sitting beside him. "It's McCoy and Billy. They followed us here."

"How could they have found us?" asked Kate anxiously.

"Remember, back in Fort Benton you mentioned that we were going to Kohrs' Ranch."

"But why, Jamie? Why did they follow us?"

"I dunno. They scare me a little."

When they told Patrick that they thought McCoy and Billy had been inquiring about them at the ranch, he dismissed it.

"It's a free country. They can go wherever they want."

But Jamie and Kate were worried. What would those outlaws do next?

Josh gave the two young wranglers a hand to gather the horses and soon they had thirty-five ponies milling around in the pasture. One of the horses was the black stallion.

"You might as well take that stallion with you," Chisholm told him. "Seems like you're the only one who can ride him."

When Jamie told Patrick that they had the horses ready he found a worried man. "I've got to pay for the cattle and now the horses. Then I've got the wages of the men. I don't know how I'm going to do it, Jamie. The money I brought with me is barely enough to pay for the food that we need."

The boy didn't know what to say to him. Patrick should have thought about all of this before they set out for Montana, but now it was too late. They were committed to driving this herd up into Canada, and all they could do was hope that they would get enough money to pay the debts by selling off the steers when they got there.

But Patrick did not let his worries show to any of the others. Mister Patrick is what he was now called by the cowboys, and he wore his new name as a badge of distinction. Jamie was known as "boy," and they called Kate, "girl." Almost everyone in the crew had a nickname that they had earned, but Kate and Jamie's names seemed to suggest that they had yet to win distinction of any kind.

But it was the cattle that Patrick thought most about. As they were brought down from the hills he examined each one carefully. These were shorthorn cattle that had been brought by Kohrs from the ranges in Oregon, Idaho and Utah, not the Texas longhorns from the south. The shorthorns were quieter and fatter than the tough wily longhorns, but they needed watching all the same.

By the evening of the fourth day in the camp, their herd had been selected, the horses gathered and the crew signed on. They were ready to move out. After supper of stew and biscuits Josh wandered over to where Jamie and Kate were talking.

"I was thinkin' about yer gear," he said slowly.

"What about it?" Jamie asked.

"Well you ain't properly fitted for the drive. I expected Mister Patrick was gonna buy an outfit for you, but it seems like he ain't. Same as you there, girl, you'se needs a better outfit or you're gonna be mighty uncomfortable on the trail. The two of you best come with me."

Josh led them to the chuck wagon and spoke to the cook. He carried everything that a cowboy needed. Soon they were given rain slickers, a good sturdy rope, spurs and chaps for their legs.

"Who's gonna pay for all this?" asked the cook.

"Put it onto Mister Patrick's tab," replied the cowboy.

Jamie felt a sudden panic. More expenses, but what could they do? They needed proper gear.

"Do you need a six-shooter, boy?" Josh asked.

"I've got my rifle."

"Yer a long way away from anythin' out there. Sometimes a man needs a weapon."

"In Canada we don't carry guns."

"Suit yourself. But you do need this." Josh took two cowboy hats out of the chuck wagon and gave one to each of them. "No self respectin' cowboy is out on the range without a hat. Keeps the sun off you in the summer and the rain off you in the fall and spring and the snow off yer head in the winter. Every man's got to have a good hat."

7

The next morning the cattle drive began. Before dawn the cowboys got up, dressed, ate, and were in the saddle. It was a beautiful June day. The pasture was green and lush, and a mist rose off the land into the clear blue sky. As the sun came over the horizon it showed the green and brown patches of the lovely Deer Lodge Valley and gleamed off the snow on the tops of the mountains.

The cowboys took up their positions, and the herd began to stir. The animals got to their feet in a soundless motion as if they knew that something important was about to happen. Patrick, the trail boss, was out in front. On the point on either side of the herd were Chisholm and Josh. Behind them, riding flank, were Buck and Mike and riding drag, at the rear of the herd, were Trapper and Fergie. Jamie and Kate rode with the horses towards the rear, on the left flank. Jamie was riding the stallion. It was still half-wild, but he knew that it was the best horse that they had.

"Ho cattle, ho!" Patrick called out, and the call was passed from man to man. "Ho cattle, ho, ho, ho!" The cowboys began squeezing the cattle into a long line, pressing them forward slowly and patiently, heading off the strays before they wandered from the herd. The animals began to move forward, grazing as they walked. They followed Patrick along a trail that followed the stream, heading down into the valley towards Kohrs' Ranch.

Soon the herd of cattle was strung out in a line five or six abreast and half a mile long. The steers gathered out in front of the herd. They were the strongest and most orderly. The cows and their calves, coming up behind, were easily distracted. Calves often bolted away and had to be chased back into the herd. The cows looked around anxiously searching for their offspring. It took all the efforts of the cowboys to keep them in line.

Towards noon Patrick found some good pasture. He signalled to the others, and the herd came to a stop. Some of the cattle went to the stream to have a drink, and others began to graze while the men took a break to eat their dinner. Two of the cowboys rode around the herd to keep them in order and head off any strays. Jamie and Kate drove the horses into the corral made up of two strands of rope.

"I'm going on ahead to the ranch," Patrick explained over their meal. "I've got to hire on a cook, and there's papers to be signed. Bring the herd into the pasture close to the ranch. I'll meet you there at sundown." He rode off in a hurry as soon as he had finished eating.

The rest of the day was uneventful. They moved the herd slowly, letting the animals graze as they went. They seemed to be a placid, easy-to-manage group of cattle. By six in the evening they had arrived at the pasture close to the ranch. They had travelled the first ten miles of the drive without an incident.

The cowboys had settled around the campfire when a procession of horses, wagons and people began to arrive. First came the chuck wagon driven by a Chinese cook by the name of Lee. He was getting things organized even before he drew his team of horses to a halt. "All right, where's that there girl they call Kate? What's a female doin' on a cattle drive anyway?"

Kate and Jamie both hurried to help the new cook. He was not the type of man you would want to be upset with you. But the cowboys were happy to see Lee. He had the reputation of being the best camp cook in the district.

Shortly afterwards Patrick returned, filled with excitement. When he caught Jamie alone he couldn't help but brag of his accomplishments. "It's all in here, signed, sealed and delivered." He patted the saddlebags to show where he was keeping the papers. "All I need is to get a good price for the steers, and then I'll be solvent again." Jamie did not want to remind him that that was only part of the worry.

The cowboys were eating supper of stew and biscuits when the rest of the procession arrived. Augusta Kohrs, sitting sidesaddle aboard a brown mare, was dressed in a splendid outfit with a high-necked, dark brocaded gown that showed the white petticoats at her ankles. Around her shoulders was a beautiful handmade lace shawl. Her dark hair was parted in the centre and pulled into a bun at the back of her head. Around her neck was a gold chain with a beautiful pendant. Her earrings and rings were diamonds and sapphires.

Her husband, Conrad, dressed in a black suit with a broad-brimmed hat, and carrying a gold-headed cane, leaped to the ground and helped his wife dismount. As rich and powerful as he was, this was a man who would do anything for the woman he loved.

Ignoring the dust and dirt that might spoil her beautiful outfit, Augusta joined the men sitting around the fire. She called to Kate, who was helping the cook, to come and talk to her. The cowboys, nervous at this noble presence who had come into their midst, hurried to get a saddle for her to sit on so she would not spoil her gown.

Before settling, Augusta made a grand pronouncement to all the assembled cowboys, like a queen addressing her nation. "I want every man here to look out for this girl. If anything happens to Kate then you'd better not come close to Kohrs' Ranch again or I'll have your hide for a pin cushion."

Kate and Augusta chatted away again like sisters. They were two female adventurers in a man's world. Jamie felt uneasy interrupting them, but he knew that he must.

"Ah, Miss Augusta?" She looked up at him. "Did two men stop by and ask for us?"

"Why yes, and they were most rude and impolite. They pounded on the front door of the ranch house like they didn't care about anyone or anything. One was young. About your age, Jamie, poorly dressed, dirty and tired. The other was in his twenties. There was something odd about him. He carried two guns, like he expected trouble, one in a holster and the other stuck in his belt."

"Did they ask for us?"

"Yes. They knew your names and everything. When I told them that you were up in the high country they just left. Just rode away in the opposite direction without a thank-you. Do you know who they are?"

"Yes, I think so." Jamie moved away before she could ask any more questions.

It was a pleasant evening, but when the sun went down, the Kohrs went back to their ranch house and the cowboys were soon in their bedrolls. They started out on their drive the next morning as the dawn broke over the mountains to the east. Slowly they began moving the herd down a trail that led past the house, the corrals, bunkhouses and sheds that made up the Kohrs' Ranch headquarters.

Kate rode with Jamie, herding the horses. As they went past the ranch house Augusta came out onto the front porch of the big white house and waved to them. Kate rode her horse over to the white picket fence that surrounded the house. She tipped her broad-brimmed cowboy hat in greeting. "I'll write," the young girl called out.

"Be careful, Kate," Augusta called back.

"Thanks for everything." Kate waved, then turned her horse and rode back to the herd. When they were about to pass the last of the buildings of the ranch she looked back to see Augusta still watching them from the verandah and then she was gone from sight.

That night they stopped by the Little Blackfoot River where the cattle had good grazing and plenty of water. Over supper Patrick told the crew what they could expect. "The next couple of days, going over the MacDonald Pass, will be the worst part of the trip."

The prediction was accurate. The trail followed the river up into the mountains. At first the grade was easy, and in the morning they made good time, but by early afternoon it had narrowed down to a dirt track hemmed in with thick pine forests. The herd could travel no more than three abreast, and the cowboys had little room to manoeuvre their horses. The cattle did not like the confined space of the trail or the cowboys pushing them on, but there was no place for them to escape.

Patrick had gone to scout ahead. In the late afternoon they came across a pasture, but he would not let them rest for the night. They pressed on for another two hours. When nightfall came they were trapped on the narrow mountain road. There was no grazing and, though there was water close by, the cattle could not get down to it. The cowboys could do little more than spend the night trying to keep calm among the herd of anxious, milling animals.

Chisholm was furious. "We should have stopped when we had the pasture," he told the trail boss.

Patrick was defensive. "The faster we get through the pass the better off we will be."

"The cattle need feed and water. You can't push them too hard!"

The next day was even worse. As they got close to the summit the trail became progressively steep. For hours the cowboys had to push the reluctant cattle up the trail by any means possible. Finally, at midday, they got to the top of the pass and found some good grazing land, but there was no water.

Kate rode up to help Lee with the noon meal, and overheard Patrick arguing with Chisholm and Josh.

"The cattle have to have water," the Texan was saying.

"I'll go ahead and scout the trail," Patrick replied.

"No! You stay. I'm gonna go."

"But I'm the trail boss."

It was Josh who headed off the argument. "We need you here, Mister Patrick. The men are tired. They need your support."

An hour later Chisholm returned to say that he had found good water and grazing. They would have to drive the herd some distance along the narrow trail to get there. It was going to be difficult, but the cattle had to have water before they were bedded down.

The herd was exhausted from the long climb up to the pass, but the cowboys moved them out over the treacherous trail littered with rocks and boulders. Finally, close to nightfall, they found the water and grazing pasture where the cattle could rest and fill their bellies.

It was after the herd was settled down that Chisholm sought out Jamie. "I heard you were worried about outlaws, boy."

"Did you see someone?" Kate asked anxiously.

"Believe so. Someone's followin' us, watchin' us from the hills. I can feel it."

Jamie felt panicked. "It's got to be McCoy and Billy."

The Texan studied the mountains crowding in upon them. "These hills are filled with cattle rustlers."

"Will they attack?" Kate asked.

"They'll wait 'til we're out on the open plains. But keep a wary eye, both of you. They're out there somewheres."

As they came out of the mountains, the road was easier. The trees became scarce and then disappeared altogether. The cattle were able to browse and graze, while the cowboys relaxed and set up a routine. That night over supper Patrick told them that now that they were out of the mountains they would head due north, all the way to Canada.

The next day they skirted the town of Helena and found the trail that led them along the Missouri River. For the next two days they pushed the herd of cattle through rugged, difficult hills. Finally the country opened up; they were able to get away from the river and found themselves on the open rolling plains.

It was the fourth day north of Helena that Jamie spotted Billy and McCoy, or at least he thought he spotted them. There were two horsemen on a hill in the distance. Jamie sensed there was something familiar about them and rode in their direction. One of the horsemen disappeared, but the other defiantly continued to watch from the hill. He could have been wrong, but Jamie was sure that it was Billy.

Over the noon meal he mentioned it to the others. "Did you see those two horsemen watching us from the bluff to the west?" he asked.

"Was they Indians?" Buck asked, nervously.

"They wore big hats."

"Could be outlaws," Chisholm suggested. "Cattle rustlers. There ain't no law here."

"No policemen, you mean," corrected Patrick.

"The people have to be their own policemen." There was a hardness to Chisholm's voice. "We'll string up any cattle rustler that comes our way."

"That's not the way to impose law and order," lectured the trail boss. "Justice has to be fair and open with courts and honest police officers."

Chisholm and some of the other cowboys smiled. "It's just as well that you're headin' back to Canada. This ain't no place fer a man who won't use his gun."

"Vigilante justice is no justice at all," concluded Patrick.

The group of cowboys had grown silent. The men held opposing points of views. There could be no resolution to this argument.

"I thought I recognized that person on the hill," Jamie said into the silence.

"Who was it?" asked Patrick.

"He was a long way away, and I couldn't be sure, but the one who stayed the longest could have been Billy."

This got the attention of the trail boss. "Billy? Are you sure?"

"He was too far away."

"Who's Billy?" Josh asked.

"Billy and McCoy. We knew them up in Canada," Patrick explained. "They were trouble."

"Loosen yer guns, there boys," said Chisholm. "Never know what a man's got to do in this country."

The conversation had put the men on edge. The country was emptier now: rolling grasslands and big blue sky. To the west of them were mountain ranges, and to the east the land stretched into the distance for as far as the eye could see. As they rode, Jamie and Kate watched the hills around them, looking for strange horsemen in the distance, but there was little sign of life.

Once they were on the open plains a routine was set up. Two lead steers, selected by Chisholm, set the pace for the herd. Behind them came the rest of the steers, and following them were the cows and calves. Soon after the drive began in the morning the herd strung out into a long line about four or five abreast. They moved steadily, grazing as they went. After the noon meal the cowboys picked up the pace to a steady walk that ate up the miles. By the time nightfall came, and the herd had settled to graze, they had covered a good ten miles or more.

Through the night two men had to ride watch on the herd at all times. Every man, Jamie included, took his turn. The cowboys would select a horse for their watch and stake it close to where they slept so that when their turn came they could easily saddle their mount and be on their way.

On the same day that Jamie had spotted the two horsemen in the distance Kate asked him if he would help her with the supper dishes. The boy was to ride the midnight watch, and he was so tired from the full day in the saddle that all he wanted was to collapse into his bedroll right after eating.

"I'm too tired, Kate," he pleaded.

"You promised, Jamie, but you haven't helped since we left Deer Lodge."

"But I've got to get up in about two hours to do my watch," the boy replied.

"But that's what you said."

"All right."

The boy had his hands in sudsy warm water, washing the dishes, pots and pans, when Kate asked, "How do you think the drive is going?"

"I'm worried about Patrick. He's made a lot of mistakes."

"I know." The two of them were speaking quietly so that no one would overhear them.

"Everything should have been planned out to the last detail before we left."

His sister laughed. "If he'd done that we would never have left Canada."

Jamie smiled. "I guess that's right. Patrick seems to think everything is easy."

"What do you think?"

"Nothing's easy in this country."

That night Josh woke the boy around midnight so that they could begin their watch. Jamie found it hard to shake himself awake, but reluctantly he climbed out of his bedroll and carried his saddle over to the gelding that he had staked close by. The horse was older and more placid than most of the semi-wild animals that cowboys rode. Jamie knew he needed a reliable mount on the night rides. In a moment the boy was into the saddle.

The moon was still not up, and the clear night sky was brilliant with billions of stars that provided a continuous canopy over their heads. Josh paused for a moment before they began their rounds to point out the Big Dipper and the North Star.

"If you can spot them you'll never lose your direction, and you'll always know the time, boy," he said with his southern accent.

"How do you mean?" Jamie asked.

"Watch closely and you'll see that the North Star doesn't move in the sky, but the Dipper and all the other stars swing around it. That's how cowboys tell time at night."

But there was no more time to talk. Josh headed out to circle the herd in a clockwise direction, and Jamie headed the other way around aboard his gelding. Soon the boy heard his partner singing a haunting southern spiritual, a song of former slaves.

Cowboys always sang as they watched the herd at night. It gave the cattle comfort to know that someone was out there looking after them. Some of the cowboys claimed that the animals even knew the difference between singers and different songs.

As he rode Jamie began to remember all the songs he had heard over the years around campfires or while men worked. First he sang the "Red River Valley," a song about Manitoba where his family lived. Then railway songs came back to him that he had heard sung by the workers as they laboured under the hot sun. As he sang, the cattle would look up at him, chewing their cud and making contented noises. Quiet had settled on the herd.

As they ended their watch Josh asked if he had been looking at the stars.

"I guess I was singing and forgot," Jamie replied.

Josh pointed at the northern sky. "See how the Big Dipper has moved about?"

It was true. In the two hours of their watch the North Star had kept its position, but the Big Dipper had rotated so that it was lower in the sky and more upright. Jamie knew that the movement was the result of the rotation of the earth.

"If you watch nature you'll never be lost and never lonely," the big man said as he slipped into his bedroll.

A few hours later, they were on the move again. There was no trail to lead them north, and they found few signs of humans, but there was wildlife in abundance. Elk and antelope bounded away as soon as the herd loomed into sight. There were gophers, grouse and prairie chicken. Often they would spot wolves watching the herd, waiting for any weak strays that they could attack. Overhead, lone eagles and hawks watched the procession of the herd.

The days were hot now. The sun blazed down making cattle, horses and humans sweat. Grasshoppers stirred up in big clouds as the cattle moved through the grass. During the day bull flies the size of bees buzzed overhead attacking animals and humans alike. Sweat seemed to attract them. The cattle and horses would toss their heads and sometimes break into a run to try and get away, but the persistent insects attacked again and again, biting and pestering the animals.

In the hot July nights swarms of mosquitoes descended upon the cowboys as they tried to sleep. Everyone was covered in bites. Kate's face swelled up, and Jamie found he just couldn't sleep unless he crowded so close to the fire that he suffered from the smoke.

In the day everyone spent their time slapping at the bull flies or waving their big hats to try and get rid of them. A bite from one of the flies was painful and left a big welt. By midafternoon blood from the bites had crusted at the backs of their necks and other vulnerable places. But still they pressed on.

One early afternoon the wind picked up, swirling the dust into tight little miniature tornadoes. In the east big clouds gathered in the sky, reaching thousands of feet into the air. Birds fluttered off, heading for shelter, but the humid heat only encouraged the bull flies to attack more viciously.

Patrick had been a long way ahead of the herd, scouting for water. He returned at a gallop. "Bed them down here!" he shouted to Chisholm and Josh. "There's a storm coming! I want every man to ride watch until it passes!"

Now the clouds in the east extended across the whole sky and were transformed into a black, angry, boiling mass that rumbled uneasily. The cowboys circled out, letting the cattle graze, but the animals were nervous and jumpy. More than one made a bolt for freedom and had to be headed off and driven back into the herd.

Lightening suddenly split the air and the thunder came seconds later, rolling and rumbling across the barren foothills. Then another bolt of lightening struck and more thunder. The black storm clouds surged in turmoil all around them. Hard driving rain in big drops began to pelt down, and an instant later a torrential downpour came out of the turbulent sky.

The herd was spooked. Steers and cows were milling about, terrified by the thunder and lightening. There was another big thunderclap, and a young calf close by Jamie made a sudden bolt for freedom. Other cattle were close behind. Jamie raced his horse to head them off. He knew he had to get out in front of them and turn them back or the whole spooked herd would follow.

Jamie was riding his half-wild stallion. He raked its ribs with his heels, and the horse responded instantly. In several powerful strides the stallion was out in front of the calf, cutting it off, forcing it back towards the rest of the milling herd. The other breakouts followed behind.

Chisholm rode up to Jamie. The two cowboys had their slickers pulled over their shoulders. Their big hats poured with water, giving them some protection, but they were still soaked. The Texan shouted something to Jamie. "Stampede ..." was all he could hear over the pounding torrent of rain.

"What's that?"

"Watch out for them cattle goin' on a stampede, boy! They're fast. Get in front of 'em. Head 'em off. Don't let 'em get away or we'll be chasin' the critters over half the territory." Then he was gone to warn the next man before Jamie could tell him that he had already headed off one stampede.

For an hour or more the heavy rain pounded down. Then the lightening and thunder passed off towards the south, and the herd gradually quieted. Soon the rain had slowed into a soft drizzle. The sun peaked out through the clouds and a rainbow appeared in the east. Everywhere lay pools of water, wet grass and mud as the land steamed with humid mist. The emergency was over, and the cowboys gathered by the chuck wagon to eat a damp supper that Lee managed to prepare.

Chisholm issued a warning to the others. "Those cattle are skittish now. Nervous as bull flies in summer heat. Anythin' can set off a stampede. I've seen the worst. Cattle killed and injured. Cowboys, who fell tryin' to stop 'em, pounded into pulp."

"Then we'll have to head off the stampede before it happens," said Patrick, anxious to stop the negative feeling.

"Easily said, but hard to do," drawled the Texan. "In a stampede you've got to get out in front of 'em and turn the herd back onto itself. That's somethin' only a brave man or a fool would try."

Things did seem to settle that night. The herd quieted, and the cowboys were able to get some sleep, but the next day the sun was fierce. The flies were worse than ever, driving humans and animals to distraction. There was more than one breakout as the cattle tried to get away from their tormentors. Over and over again men and horses were put to the test. Exhaustion was setting in from hours in the saddle and lack of sleep.

That night, as Jamie and Josh took their watch, a nervous restlessness had taken possession of the herd. The cattle were on their feet milling about and would not settle. The moon drifted in a sky filled with clouds making it hard to see details on the ghostly pale prairie. A strong west wind stirred the grass restlessly.

Jamie watched and listened. He was riding his stallion again. He had pushed the horse too hard in the last few days, but he wanted to be aboard his best mount on this unsettled night. For an hour they rode their watch, but still the herd had not settled.

The boy was on the far side from the camp when he thought he saw something in the distance. Then there was a noise. Jamie turned. He was sure that he saw a man waving a blanket to frighten the herd. Instantly the nervous cattle were on the move. It was a breakout! A stampede!

8

Jamie let out the cry, "Stampede! Stampede!"

The cattle were terrified, their eyes bugging from their heads, and yet the herd was strangely soundless. There were no bellows, no frightened, frantic moos. Not a beast uttered a sound except for the thunder of their hooves, but that alone was enough to spread panic. The ground gave a deep rumbling, a trembling, that felt like an earthquake about to shake the very foundations of the world.

In the camp, where the cowboys were sleeping, Patrick listened. Suddenly he was on his feet. "Stampede!" he shrieked. "Stampede! All hands into the saddle! Stampede!"

The cowboys were out of their bedrolls, racing for their night horses that they had staked close by. Kate had sensed that there might be trouble. She had left her saddle on her buffalo pony and staked it near her. It took only a moment for her to run for her mount and leap into the saddle.

The cattle were in full stampede back along the trail they had come. They ran with surprising speed, hooves pounding on the hard earth, horns clashing as they thundered on. The herd raced blindly, running as hard as they could to get away from whatever it was that had given fright in the first place. There was no thought, no reason, only the blinding chaos of a wild herd in full flight.

Jamie raked the sides of his stallion with his heels. He knew that he had to get out in front of the herd and turn them in order to stop their panicked, thundering flight. The stampede was well out in front of him. This was no time to think of the man with the blanket, no time to worry about himself.

He had to stop the stampede. This was his watch, his responsibility.

The boy kicked the sides of his stallion again. There were raging cattle on all sides of him. If his horse stumbled Jamie knew he would be trampled to death by the animals' sharp hooves within seconds. But he would not stop. He had to trust his horse.

The darkness was all about, but the moon came out from behind the clouds enough to show the racing, frightened herd running with every ounce of strength in their powerful bodies. As he raced with the cattle he felt heat rise off them, hot enough to blister his face. But still they galloped on. Horses, steers, cows and calves raced in a frantic wild run that left any thought of safety behind, but he was gaining on the herd. Even with all the panic of the cattle, Jamie's stallion was faster.

Kate was well back of the herd. At first her buffalo pony was frightened and ran outside the stampeding herd. Her horse could see the flashing horns of the cattle and shied away from them. She spurred her mount, and it began to run at the pace of the herd. She saw other cowboys. Some stayed well back, frightened of being caught in the thundering herd, but others rode hard for the leaders in an attempt to stop the stampede.

Jamie could not think about what was going on behind him. He knew the stallion was his only hope to get out in front of the cattle. He gave his horse its head and crouched low over its neck so that horse and rider were one streamlined racing unit. The stallion ran as if he knew that both their lives depended on getting out in front of the herd. One mile, two miles, maybe three, they ran. The boy and his horse would not give up on this desperate chase, and the herd showed no signs of slowing.

But they were winning this reckless race. Jamie could see the leaders of the stampeding herd now. He was almost out in front. Then he noticed Josh not far behind him. They were both racing hard for the front of the herd.

Finally the boy and his horse were abreast of the panicked steers who were leading this wild stampede. This was the most dangerous moment. Jamie had to turn the leaders so that the whole herd would follow and run in a circle. He eased his horse over. The stallion give a bump to the steer running in the lead. The steer began to move to the right. The animal turned and other cattle coming behind followed.

Jamie could see Josh a few strides behind. Both of them were forcing the cattle to move into a big arc. It was working. In the pale moonlight Jamie could see how the still stampeding herd was circling. It took terrifying minutes of reckless hard riding, but finally the leaders of the herd had circled around, meeting others that were in the tail of the stampede.

There was confusion. The leaders merged with those that were coming behind. Animals bumped into each other, stopped running, and began milling about. In a moment the hard-racing herd was no more than a confusing mass of mooing, braying cattle. The stampede was over. Jamie and his stallion found themselves in the middle of this mass of dazed and bewildered cattle. He took his hat off to wipe his brow and feel the cool night air. Finally he could feel the tension from this wild race ease away.

The black stallion was lathered in sweat, breathing heavily, its body trembling. Jamie leaned over and stroked the silky black neck of his mount. "You're the best," he whispered into the stallion's ear. "You stopped the stampede."

"You're some cowboy." Josh was smiling beside him. The cattle milled about them.

"It was my black stallion that did it."

"A horse is important, but it's the man in the saddle that makes the difference."

They began to ride slowly out of the crowd of milling cattle. The other cowboys had already taken up positions around the herd to head off the possibility of another stampede. Some had started to sing to help quiet the animals.

"What do you think spooked them?" Josh asked.

"I'm sure I saw someone down by the herd waving a blanket."

"Really? You mean someone stampeded them on purpose? Who was it?"

"I couldn't see him. It was too dark," said Jamie.

"Chisholm," Josh called. The Texan cowboy rode up to them. "The boy here says that he thinks that someone spooked the herd by waving a blanket at them."

"Rustlers! It's got to be rustlers. They stampede the herd and then drive off the stragglers while the cowboys chase the rest. We've got to tell the trail boss."

They found Patrick with other cowboys trying to make a survey of the herd. The sun was beginning to lighten the eastern horizon. "It's a disaster," the trail boss was saying. "The cattle ran maybe four miles. Some of them got gored. I saw a calf who'd broken its leg. Who knows how many got killed or trampled to death."

"Mister Patrick," said Chisholm, interrupting the trail boss. "The boy here saw somethin' you should know about."

"What's that, Jamie?"

"I was riding my watch just before the stampede began, and I saw someone waving a blanket."

"A blanket?" Patrick was puzzled.

"Someone wanted to spook the herd and start a stampede," Josh explained.

"Rustlers" concluded Chisholm with a hard edge to his voice. "They are all through these hills, and they're just lookin' for a chance to make off with cattle."

"Well, they will not rustle my herd!" Patrick announced emphatically. "I won't put up with it."

"Once we settle down the herd we'll get a group of the boys and go after them," said the Texan cowboy. "They can't be far. A little rope for a necktie. That's what makes these outlaws take notice."

Patrick knew exactly what that meant. "There will be no frontier justice while I am the trail boss here!"

"That's what they deserve!"

"As I said before, I was a police officer, and I won't tolerate my men becoming vigilantes. We'll bring them to trial."

"Where?" demanded Chisholm. "There ain't a judge within a hundred miles of here."

"I'm the trail boss of this outfit." Patrick was dead serious. "No one gets strung up while I'm in charge. Do you understand, Chisholm?"

There was a long pause before the cowboy nodded. "You make yerself real clear."

"Good. I'm going to look after this myself. I've handled worst situations when I was in the North West Mounted Police, and a little cattle rustling doesn't worry me."

Chisholm and Josh looked at each other but said nothing. Patrick was the trail boss, and his word was law.

Patrick turned his horse and started riding back towards the camp. "Jamie, I want you to show me exactly where you saw this person waving the blanket. And Chisholm ..." He reined in and called back over his shoulder, "Hold the herd here. We won't drive today. Get them settled down. I don't want another stampede. You had best send some men out to

see if they can find any strays. I'll send Lee and the chuck
wagon back to give you some breakfast."

"Yes, sir."

Jamie and Kate rode with Patrick back along the trail
pounded down by the stampeding herd. It was a sad sight.
They found a steer with a broken leg that had to be put out of
its misery, and two calves lost from their mothers. Jamie
roped the calves so they would not wander away and led them
behind his horse back to the camp.

Lee, the cook, had already got his outfit together. He had
picked up all of the belongings of the men that had been
scattered around the camp and put them in the back of the
chuck wagon. Patrick told the cook to take the chuck wagon
over to the herd and then concluded by saying, "I'm going to
get those rustlers."

"You gonna go alone, Mister Patrick?" the cook asked.

"I'm not afraid of some petty criminals."

"It's a mighty wild country out there. Lots of bad men
with plenty of weapons."

The trail boss ignored the comment but whispered to
Jamie, "Some people are too frightened to do anything."

The cook went on his way with the two calves following
behind, tied to the back of his chuck wagon.

Jamie led Patrick and Kate to the spot where he remembered seeing the person with the blanket. There was nothing
there they could find. The three of them scouted a wider and
wider area until Jamie came across hoof prints leading away
from the herd up into the foothills to the west of them. He called
to the others and got off his horse to examine the ground. It was
the hoof prints of cattle all right. Then they spotted the prints of
horses. There was one at least, perhaps two.

"It looks like someone drove these cattle away," concluded Patrick. "Perhaps twenty-five or thirty head is my
guess."

"Do you think they were stolen, Patrick?" Kate asked.

"There can be no doubt about that."

"What are you going to do?"

"It won't be hard to follow their trail. I'm going after them."

"Don't you think that's risky?" asked Jamie.

Patrick laughed. "Are you afraid like the others?"

"Chisholm said that the outlaws around here are dangerous."

"What does Chisholm know about bandits? I've arrested more in my lifetime than he's ever met."

"But this is not like Canada, Patrick. The men here are all armed, and they use their weapons."

"I can look after myself. I've got my Winchester and my revolver." He patted the gun he carried at his waist. "The longer I wait the more of a head start they will have."

"Maybe we should come with you," Kate said, feeling very uneasy.

"You'd just hold me back. Don't worry. I'm a trained policeman. I'll be back soon with those outlaws and the cattle. We'll bring those men to justice."

"Be careful," Kate called after him.

Patrick rode off, following the trail of the cattle up into the hills. When he was a little distance away he reined in and turned to call out one last message. "Go back and help the others. We can't afford another stampede. I'm counting on the two of you to help me get this herd back to Canada." Then he spurred his mount, and in a moment he had disappeared over the top of the hill.

They rode the four miles back to the herd without talking. Both Kate and Jamie were concerned about Patrick. He should not be heading alone out into that wild country. Who knew what would be waiting for him? The drive was not going well. Stampedes, bad weather, insects and restless cowboys. What else could go wrong?

Already they were tired. Jamie felt an ache deep down in his body from lack of sleep. Spending sixteen hours or more in the saddle every day was wearing him down. He had hardly slept the night before.

Kate at least could sleep through the nights. She was not required to stand watch, like her brother, but she was not used to these unending hours spent in the hot sun and labouring all hours of the day or night.

When they got back to the herd they found Lee had made a camp under a small growth of dogwood near a creek. Both of them were eating when Josh and Chisholm rode in.

The men poured themselves coffee as Chisholm explained. "We did a count and figure twenty-five head are missing. Another two were killed in the stampede along with a couple of calves. We looked everywhere for the twenty-five but they're gone."

"We found traces of the missing cattle near where we bedded them down last night," Jamie explained. "Patrick's gone out after them."

"Alone?" asked Josh.

"We begged him not to go, but he wouldn't listen," said Kate.

Chisholm shook his head. "Should never travel alone in this country. You never know what you're gonna meet."

Jamie felt uneasy. He could not rest. Soon he was up on his horse again helping the men ride watch. The cattle were still skittish. Chisholm had warned everyone that they had to be extra watchful the next few days. Once a herd stampedes it is likely that they will do it again.

But it was not the herd that the boy was worried about. He was thinking of Patrick up in the hills, following the trail of cattle driven by who knows what type of ruthless outlaws. He shouldn't have gone alone. Maybe they should have insisted that they go with him, but how could they stop him? The boy tormented himself with these thoughts as he rode on the outskirts of the herd keeping watch.

The sun rose into the sky overhead. There was still no sign of Patrick. What could have happened to him? Was he bushwhacked by some outlaw? Maybe he had fallen. Maybe he had recovered the cattle and was having trouble bringing them back. Finally he could not stand it any longer and rode over to where Josh and Chisholm were talking.

"He's been gone a long time," the boy started.

"Too long," said Chisholm.

"We're thinkin' that maybe we'd best go out and see if we can give Mister Patrick a hand," added Josh.

"I'm sure he's fine," said Jamie. "Maybe he just needs a hand to bring in the cattle."

The big cowboy nodded. "That's probably true. Why don't you show us the last spot that you saw him, and we'll go and look for that trail boss of ours."

9

"Jamie, Josh and I are goin' to find Mister Patrick," Chisholm told the other cowboys as they collected their gear.

"Be careful," replied Buck. "It's a wild country out there."

Kate was upset. "I'm going with you."

"You'd best stay here with the others," said Chisholm.

But Kate would not hear of it. "Patrick's our friend. I'm coming along."

Chisholm knew there was no point in arguing with the headstrong girl. In a few minutes they had their things together, and the four of them rode out of camp on their mission to find the trail boss.

Jamie led them to the spot where they had last seen Patrick. Chisholm and Josh got off their horses to study the hoof prints. "It's rustlers all right," Chisholm announced, after a careful examination of the ground. "I reckon they've got about twenty-five head of cattle, and they're drivin' them hard. There's hoof prints of three horses. One has to belong to Mister Patrick so there's two outlaws."

"What are you going to do when you find them?" Kate asked anxiously.

"*If* we find them. They've got a big lead, and this is a big country. Let's go. We've got a lot of ground to cover."

The twenty-five rustled cattle left a trail through the grass as broad as a small river. It led uphill, west, towards the mountains. The slope was hard on horses, but the four riders pressed them. They were worried now. None of them spoke of it, but they knew that the outlaws must have planned their raid well in advance. They were going to be prepared for anyone pursuing them.

Soon the trail led into the high country of meadows and pine and aspen forests. They had been riding an hour when Chisholm held his hand up for them to rein in. "Be on your guard now," the Texan told the others. "They've got the higher ground. There's a good chance they'll see us comin'."

"How far do you figure they are ahead of us?" Jamie asked.

"Hard to say. Josh answered. We're travelling a lot faster than they can move with the cattle, but they've got a good head start."

They were off again, riding as hard as they could. Josh and Chisholm led the way, but Kate and Jamie were close behind. Their horses were strong, and they were eating up the miles. After another hour the Texan brought them to a halt again.

"We'll give the horses a rest. Jamie, Kate, get the food organized." Chisholm spoke in a short, clipped way. He was focused on the business at hand and had no time for small talk.

When Kate was taking the food from her saddlebags she noticed the two cowboys had taken out their guns and were inspecting them to see that they were fully loaded and in working order.

"Best take a look at your Winchester, there boy," Chisholm said in that quiet determined way that he had.

"Are you going to have to use the guns?" Kate asked. She felt uneasy.

"If there's trouble you stay back, girl," Chisholm ordered. "I don't want you gettin' mixed up in none of this."

Jamie took out his rifle from its long holster on the saddle. It was fully loaded. The barrel was clean, ready for use. He got all of the extra cartridges that he carried and put them into the pocket of his shirt. He felt a strange anxiety. He had never been on a hunt like this before.

When they started again Josh and Chisholm held their rifles with the butt on their thigh and the barrels pointing upwards. Jamie did the same. The boy felt a strange tingling feeling down the back of his neck. He sensed that they were walking into danger.

The land was broken into hills and high bluffs. There were groves of trees mixed with open meadows. The outlaws would know that anyone pursuing them would be following their trail. All they had to do was hide and wait for them to come.

Despite their concerns, they rode hard, pushing their horses to the limit of their strength and endurance. The trail they were following was still leading upwards into the high country. Maybe the outlaws had a hideout somewhere up in the hills. Maybe they had mounted a guard and were waiting for them on the trail.

The four horses and riders were crossing a broad meadow. In the distance was a stream coming out of the hills, and beyond the stream was an aspen grove. That was when Kate spotted Patrick's horse. She pointed. "There ... there up near the wood on the other side of the stream!"

Patrick's favourite mount was grazing in the meadow. The horse still had its saddle on, and the reins dangled uselessly on the ground. There was no sign of the trail boss.

Jamie spurred his mount and splashed through the stream. Josh shouted to him to come back. It was too dangerous to expose himself like that, but the boy did not care. He raced with all of the strength left in his stallion. And then he found him. Patrick was sprawled face down on the trail. A bullet had gone clear through his chest and out the other side. There was not a sign of life in the body.

Jamie felt as if the pain of the bullet had torn through his chest. "Patrick!" he shrieked. "Patrick!" but the only reply was the echo of his own voice. In that moment he knew that their friend was utterly, completely dead.

The boy was off his horse and kneeling beside the body when the others rode up. Tears had welled up in his eyes and were pouring down his face. They had ridden a long way with this man. No matter what his faults, he was their friend. Now he was dead.

Kate knelt beside her brother and put her hand on his shoulder. She, too, began to cry. The worst possible thing had happened. Patrick was dead. Their feeling of desolation overwhelmed them. How could they go on?

They cried until the complete emptiness they felt inside left them with no tears. Finally Kate and Jamie got to their feet and joined the others. Josh and Chisholm were still on their horses, their rifles pointing at anything that looked like hidden dangers, fingers resting on the triggers.

"He was bushwhacked," Josh said quietly. "The man who shot him was waitin' up in them trees. Mister Patrick rode right into his gun sights. He didn't have a chance. It was cold-blooded murder."

The two cowboys were grim with raw anger and determination. "He was a good man," said Chisholm with a frightening calmness. "We're goin' to get the killers dead or alive. We want you two young ones to stay here with the body. We'll be back."

"I'm coming with you," said Jamie. He felt a special calm anger that came from a desire for revenge.

"Stay here, boy," ordered Josh.

"No!" Jamie said emphatically. "I'm coming. Patrick was my friend. I want to bring in his murderer." He climbed on his horse.

The two cowboys could see that there was no stopping him. "All right," said Chisholm. "But Kate, you stay. Someone needs to be with the body. We'll be back soon."

Without another word the three horsemen spurred their mounts, and they were off at a gallop, leaving Kate standing beside the dead man. She watched them disappear into the aspen grove with a sinking feeling of complete desolation.

The girl was alone in this wild country filled with outlaws. As she came to realize her situation fear began to seize her. Who was out in the hills? Were there cattle rustlers watching her from behind every tree? She didn't even have a weapon to defend herself.

When Kate looked at the body of Patrick, she began to cry again. She didn't want to stay there. She couldn't stay there. The place was too sad, too tragic. How could she stay with this dead man that she had come to care about and respect? How could she bare the sense of incredible loneliness and emptiness that she felt? Slowly she mounted her horse and began to follow the others into the aspen grove and beyond.

Jamie, Chisholm and Josh rode hard, following the trail left by the cattle. All three were on edge; they held their rifles pointing at the sky as they rode, but they were ready to use them at the least sign of trouble. Each of them searched for hidden spots where an outlaw could lie in wait, but they knew they were vulnerable. They were pushing too hard to take precautions.

Jamie could not get rid of the image of Patrick sprawled out on the ground, dead from a single shot to the chest. There was no sign of struggle. One instant the trail boss was riding along, and the next he was dead with a bullet through the chest. The killers must pay, Jamie thought to himself. He would make them pay no matter what the risks.

They had been riding hard for half an hour when Chisholm put his hand up for them to stop. They were in a broad meadow. The signs of the cattle suggested that the animals were growing tired. They had been pushed hard. They needed water and a chance to rest. The herd had spread out in the meadow to graze, the markings were clear, but the outlaws had pushed them on impatiently. They must be still worried that they were being followed.

"Hear that?" Josh suddenly asked.

The three of them were quiet, listening. Then the sound came again. It was a bellow of an angry steer some distance away. They were closing in on the stolen cattle.

"Let's get them," said Jamie impatiently.

"Wait, boy." Chisholm had become the leader of this hunt, and they waited for his orders. "We're not gonna make the same mistake as Mister Patrick. They'll be watchin' the trail and waitin' for us. We need to circle around and wait for them to walk into our trap."

"Yeah," agreed Josh. "They're gonna be so busy with that herd they won't see what's comin'."

"How far do you figure they're up ahead of us, Josh?" Chisholm asked.

"By the sounds of those cattle I'd judge no more than a couple of miles."

"You circle to the left of the herd. The boy and I will go to the right. Keep hidden and well away from their trail so they don't see you. We'll wait until they come with the herd, and then we'll jump them. Remember, there's two of them, and they ain't afraid to use their weapons."

They separated. Josh went to the left, keeping inside the trees in order to stay out of sight, while the others went to the right. Chisholm led the way through a stand of trees and then began a large encircling movement. Jamie followed close behind.

They rode hard. Occasionally Chisholm would hold up his hand, and they would rein in to listen for sounds of the cattle. The herd was some distance off, but it was clear that they were coming abreast of them. A while later they stopped and listened again. Now they were out in front of the herd.

Chisholm climbed off his horse and tried to peer through the trees. Jamie joined him. The cattle were close now. Perhaps they were on the other side of the thicket in open country. Without a word Chisholm began walking through the trees towards the clearing, leading his horse with the reins in his hands. Jamie followed behind leading his mount.

Leaves rustled at their feet so loudly the boy was afraid the sound would betray them. Still they pressed on. They could hear the cattle more clearly now. They were mooing and braying unhappily. Then, unexpectedly, Chisholm came to the edge of the aspen grove and stopped. Jamie crept up beside him.

There, through the trees, they could see the twenty-five head of cattle that had been rustled from them. The animals had been run into exhaustion and were tramping along wearily on sore bones and muscles.

Then Jamie spotted the rider pushing them. It was Billy. He was wild looking. The boy had no hat or gloves, and he wore faded, shabby clothes. For some reason the sight of Billy came as a shock to Jamie. But things were happening too quickly for him to take time to think.

"I ... I know him!" Jamie stuttered.

"There was two of them!" Chisholm whispered impatiently. "Do you see the other one?"

The boy looked everywhere. Billy was pushing the twenty-five head of cattle as hard as he could, but he was alone. Where was McCoy?

"Damn!" Chisholm looked about, considering his options. "He's gettin' past us. I'm goin' after this one with the cattle. You stay here until I get back. Stay under cover, you understand?"

Jamie nodded. A moment later Chisholm was gone, leading his horse back through the aspens. It looked like he was going to circle out in front of Billy and the cattle again so that he could surprise him.

Jamie lay in the brush, watching the clearing while his horse quietly grazed on the leaves behind him. It was quiet. Occasionally he could hear the sounds of the cattle disappearing in the distance.

So much was going through his mind that he could barely make sense of it. Either Billy or McCoy had shot Patrick. They had taken their revenge for their arrest in Canada. Now Jamie understood that they were indeed outlaws, beyond any hope of redemption.

Jamie cursed himself for being so stupid. Why didn't he figure out that this was going to happen? McCoy and Billy had followed them to Kohrs' Ranch and then waited until they were weak before they struck. At the very moment when the herd was nervous, and the men were tired, they had started the stampede. He should have known that it was going to happen.

This was a double victory for Billy and McCoy. Not only had they stolen cattle, but they had used those cattle to lure Patrick to his death. Damn them, he said to himself. He should have known. The two of them were vicious murderers. He would get them if it was the last thing that he did.

The boy watched the trail, expecting to see McCoy at any moment. Where could he be? Maybe he had gone ahead to scout out a place where they could hide the cattle. If he was waiting on the trail, he would not let Billy get too far ahead of him before he rode to catch up. Then McCoy would have to ride right past him, and he would spring on him. Jamie did not care about Chisholm's orders. He was bent on revenge.

The boy waited, crouching in the bush. Time crept by. Nothing was happening. The sounds of the cattle had grown fainter. All he could hear was birds and bull flies buzzing in the clear sky. Occasionally his horse would thump his foot. He had been told to stay out of sight but nothing was happening. Now was the time to move on. McCoy must have gone on ahead. Jamie could not wait there forever. What was happening? Where were Chisholm and Josh?

He had almost given up when suddenly he saw movement. Was it a deer or an antelope? He was peering through the trees, straining to see, when Kate loomed into sight. She was riding her horse along the trail of the cattle, unaware that anything or anyone might be watching her.

Suddenly a trap was sprung. As Jamie watched out through the underbrush at his sister approaching, McCoy rode on his horse out of a clump of aspen a hundred yards away. He had his rifle pointing right at Kate. The outlaw had been watching for them on the trail all this time.

"Well ain't this real sweet," said McCoy to Kate with a strange grin on his face.

Kate shrieked in surprise. "You! It was you who killed Patrick."

The outlaw laughed. "That policeman was either stupid or just too sure of himself."

"Why did you kill him?" she demanded.

"Look what he did to Billy and me. He wouldn't listen. He got what he deserved." McCoy's horse danced around nervously.

"You won't get away with this!"

"By the time they catch up with us and find you and that dead policeman we're gonna be long gone over the mountains. It's all over for you girlie. All over." He pointed the barrel of his gun at the girl.

"Stop, McCoy! Drop it or you're a dead man!" It was Jamie. He had crept up on foot. His Winchester was levelled at the outlaw.

McCoy whirled, startled and surprised. The gun exploded in his hands, the bullet whizzing past Jamie's ear. Kate shrieked. Jamie fell backwards.

McCoy's horse reared up on its back legs in terror. The gun went off again, frightening the horse even more. Again the horse reared, throwing McCoy from its back. The outlaw hit the ground hard with his head, and the gun fell from his hands. His horse bolted. McCoy's foot was caught in a stirrup, and his body was dragged furiously along, bouncing over mounds and boulders as the horse raced in panic across the meadow.

Jamie and Kate were mesmerized by the gruesome scene. Terror held them in its iron grip and they were unable to move.

The horse continued to run hard, dragging the body, galloping all the faster in an attempt to rid itself of that thing that bounced along behind. Finally the animal was played out and came to a stop, but there was no movement from McCoy.

"Jamie! Jamie are you all right?" Kate rushed over to her brother, tears streaming from her eyes.

The two held onto each other, frightened by events. "I'm fine, Kate. Fine ... fine," was all he could say for the moment.

The terror began to melt away. It was totally quiet in the remote meadow. They were alone now, drained of all emotions by the sheer intensity of their feelings.

Jamie picked up his Winchester. Things had happened so quickly that it was only when he looked at his rifle that he realized that it had not been discharged. Then the two of them walked across the meadow towards McCoy and his horse.

He was dead. Kate could not even look at the body, but Jamie forced himself to crouch down and look in order to make sure. No one could have survived those injuries.

It was as they were standing over the dead man that Chisholm galloped up. Josh came behind leading Billy's horse. The boy's wrists were tied to the saddle of his horse.

"We heard shots ..." Chisholm began, but when he saw the body of McCoy on the ground he grew silent.

Large scale cattle ranching on the plains grew rapidly after the American Civil War in the 1860s. It began first in Texas and moved into the northern ranges of Montana and the Canadian Foothills by the 1870s and 80s.
Montana Historical Society, Helena, 946-438

Cowboys were itinerant, poorly paid workers who moved from job to job. They often owned little more than their horse, saddle and a meager "outfit" of clothes and cooking utensils.
Montana Historical Society, Helena, 946-462

A cowboy had to have the ability to work long hours, a knowledge of cattle and above all a skill with horses. The range ponies they rode were little more than wild horses that had to be broken before they were of any use.
Montana Historical Society, Helena, 981-499

Once broken to the saddle a horse was trained to perform a variety of tasks.
National Archives of Canada, PA 189679

Though their reputation for using guns has been wildly exaggerated, many American cowboys carried weapons. In Canada the use of guns was discouraged. This unidentified cowboy is wearing woolen chaps that were used on the northern ranges in winter.
Montana Historical Society, Helena, 946-423

In the early days of ranching there were no fences and cattle were allowed to wander over a vast area of "open range." In the spring cowboys would round up the cattle and drive them to the ranches, or some other assembly point.

Montana Historical Society, Helena, 946-310

Once the cattle had been rounded up, the young calves would be branded with the ranch symbol so they could be easily identified. Mature animals would be cut out and readied for market.

National Archives of Canada, C 7835

Cattle were driven to rail heads hundreds of miles away so they could be sold and marketed. The most famous of the cattle trails was the Chisholm Trail in Texas and Oklahoma, but there were many trails in the northern ranges. Stampedes, drought and rain storms were part of the hardships of the trail. River crossings, such as this, were a special hazard.

Montana Historical Society, Helena, 946-326

On the cattle drive the cowboys ate and slept in the open air. The herd always had to be guarded and the men were in the saddle 18 hours a day.

Montana Historical Society, Helena, 946-414

The cook was one of the most important people at roundup and on the cattle drive. He prepared meals over an open fire from supplies carried in the chuck wagon. The meals were primitive: beans, salt pork, and bread, but few cowboys complained. Those that incurred the wrath of the cook might find themselves going hungry.
Montana Historical Society, Helena, 981-254

Home to a cowboy who was hired year round at a ranch would be in the bunkhouse with the other men. Some ranchers built primitive cabins like this in remote parts of the ranch for their cowboys.
National Archives of Canada, C 8813

Conrad Kohrs, a German butcher, went into ranching in Western Montana in 1868 when he bought a spread in Deer Lodge Valley. There he raised registered Shorthorns and Hereford cattle. At the height of his success Kohrs grazed herds on ten million acres of land in four states and Canada. Montana Historical Society, Helena, 943-354

Augusta Kohrs married her husband, Conrad, at the age of 19 in the year 1868. After their marriage it took the Kohrs seven weeks just to reach their ranch in Western Montana. Augusta was never afraid of hard work or hardship. She cooked, cleaned, milked cows, made soap and candies, roasted coffee, ran the house and had children. This was all part of the normal routine for women on the frontier. Montana Historical Society, Helena, 943-352

The foothills country of Canada and Montana was the territory of the Blackfoot confederacy. These nomadic people lived on buffalo and other game. An uneasy peace existed between the Blackfoot and the settlers and ranchers who moved into their territory in the latter part of the 19th century. This is a photo of a warrior called Big Moon.
Montana Historical Society, Helena, 955-428

Two Blackfoot warriors on watch. One of them carries a coup stick. A warrior who touched an enemy with a coup stick in battle, without hurting him, was given the highest honours.
National Archives of Canada, PA 41374

Crowfoot, the most important chief of the Blackfoot Nation in the troubled times at the end of the 19th century, grew up in the days of the great buffalo hunts. He witnessed the decimation of the herds and near starvation of his proud people. Through his influence peace was maintained between the Blackfoot and the whites.
National Archives of Canada, C 21815

These members of the Blackfoot Nation were already beginning to adopt western dress, but they continued to live their traditional lifestyle of nomadic hunters.
National Archives of Canada, C 1315

This is a Piegan encampment, in Montana. The Piegan, Blood and Blackfoot made up the Blackfoot Confederacy.
Montana Historical Society, Helena, 955-518

Colonel James Macleod of the North West Mounted Police, led the "red coats" into the foothills country of Canada in the summer of 1874. The Mounted Police quickly put down the trade in whiskey that had caused so much trouble for the Blackfoot. They built Fort Macleod, named after the Colonel, on an island in the Oldman River. Macleod later was appointed a magistrate.

National Archives of Canada, C 17494

This is the main street of the town of Fort Macleod in the year 1876, two years after the fort was built.
National Archives of Canada, C 19031

I. G. Baker's Grocery and Hardware store in Fort Macleod in 1885. Even after the Mounted Police drove out the American whiskey traders the area continued to be supplied by traders from Fort Benton on the Missouri River in Montana.
National Archives of Canada, C 7854

Until the North-West Rebellion of 1884 the relations between Native people and whites in Western Canada was relatively peaceful. This photo shows Crowfoot, in the left foreground, with other members of the Blackfoot Nation, a Métis trader, and a Sergeant of the North West Mounted Police.

Montana Historical Society, Helena, 955-467

This is the first photo taken in Fort Calgary in 1878. After the railway went through, Calgary became the most important centre in the foothills country.
National Archives of Canada, 8200

Crowfoot addressing the Marquis of Lorne, the Governor General of Canada, and the Blackfoot Nation.
National Archives of Canada, C 121918

10

It was a grim business. Long shadows had reached into the hills by the time they had collected the cattle and brought them back to the meadow where McCoy's body lay. A shallow grave was dug for the outlaw, and they left him in that lonely place far up in the hills, without a sign to mark the spot.

They pushed on, anxious to get out of the high country and back to the others. The three cowboys drove the cattle while Kate trailed Billy's horse with the prisoner tied to the saddle. By the time they got to the place where Patrick was shot, it was almost dark.

Jamie and Kate were completely exhausted. All they wanted to do was sleep until dawn, but there was still much to do. Josh looked after the body, wrapping it in a rain slicker, while Chisholm and Jamie rode watch on the cattle. Kate started a fire and began to heat up the little food they had left.

Since his capture no one had talked to Billy, and the boy had been surprisingly quiet. They had tied him to a tree not far from the campfire, and now, while the others were occupied, the outlaw tried to talk to Kate.

"What are they going to do with me?" he asked plaintively.

Kate studied the boy in the gathering darkness. He looked miserable. His clothes were in tatters and strain and worry marked his face. "I don't know," she replied.

"I didn't have anything to do with the killing, Kate."

"You were with McCoy."

"No, McCoy told me he was gonna check and see if anyone was tailin' us. Next thing I heard was the gunshot."

"But you were partners, and you stole the cattle with him."

Billy was quiet for what seemed like a long time before he delivered a final judgment on himself. "They're going to hang me. I can see it in your brother's eyes. They'll hang me and put me in a shallow grave just like they did with McCoy."

Kate said nothing. What could she say? She had no idea what was going to happen. A moment later she looked up to see Billy weeping.

It was a hard night. They had little to eat, each of them had to take turns riding watch on the cattle, and it was cold up in the mountains. No matter how close they got to the fire no one could get warm.

The next morning, despite their exhaustion, they headed out as the sun broke the eastern horizon. Kate led the way, trailing Billy's horse with the outlaw tied firmly to his saddle. Trailing behind them was Patrick's horse, with the body draped over the saddle. The others drove the cattle. By midday they had come out of the hills and had rejoined the herd and the rest of the crew.

The cowboys were deeply distressed to see the body of their trail boss. Patrick was laid out on the ground under a big cottonwood tree near the stream. Every man in the crew went to pay their respects, and then one by one came to give their condolences to Kate and Jamie. In the absence of family the young brother and sister had become Patrick's next of kin in the eyes of the cowboys.

In the shade of the old tree Josh dug a deep grave in the black earth of the foothills. Lee fashioned a primitive cross out of wood he took from the chuck wagon. Jamie wrote out the words he wanted on the marker on a piece of paper and Buck carved them on the horizontal piece: "Patrick McNeil, killed by outlaws, July 1877, NWMP retired, R.I.P."

The hot sun of the late afternoon beat down on the mourners as Chisholm and Josh lowered the body into the ground with their ropes. Nearby the herd grazed quietly. Grasshoppers moved in the grass near their feet and overhead a lone eagle glided soundlessly on the updrafts of the hot air rising from the land.

The men stood silently, their hats off, as the body came to rest in the grave. Kate felt tears wash over her face. Jamie had a deep sense of emptiness. Though it was hard, he knew he had to say something to mark the moment. His words were simple but deeply felt.

"Kate and I rode a long way with Patrick. No man was more honest or more fearless. He set out what he wanted to do, and he went after it. He had his failings, but he was someone you could rely on; someone who knew what was right and what was wrong; someone who would support you even when you made mistakes. He was a true friend, and we will miss him."

The wind was stirring in the big cottonwood tree as Jamie finished.

Kate added a simple postscript. "Rest peacefully Patrick. We will remember you. Rest peacefully."

They stood for a long time, and then Josh began to fill in the grave. The earth falling on the rain slicker gave a desolate sense of finality. The crew drifted away, leaving Josh to finish his task.

The cowboys were sitting around the campfire drinking coffee when Chisholm offered his solution. "I say that we should string him up."

Billy was tied to the wheel of the chuck wagon and could hear everything the cowboys were saying. When he heard those words he struggled against the ropes biting into his wrists.

Trapper, who was rarely known to speak, agreed. "We owe it to Mister Patrick."

Others were nodding. "The big cottonwood tree will hold him," said Buck.

Fear went through Jamie's body, but he said nothing. Billy strained to listen. These were tough men who sat around the fire. Their bodies were whip hard from days on the trail, and their minds were hardened by the murder of their trail boss, a man they all liked and respected.

"Let's string him up right now!" said another.

Kate felt panicked. "But ... but lynching is against the law."

"Out here we are the law," said Chisholm.

"But it's not civilized!"

"Listen, girl. There ain't no civilization in these parts." Chisholm was dead serious. "Cattlemen have to be hard, fast, ready men. To live in this country is to fight against weather, disease, fire, insects, cantankerous animals and outlaws who'll gun you down as quick as look at you. You've got to be stronger than the next man or you won't survive, and you've got to get the outlaws before they get you."

"But it's not right, Chisholm. If you take the law into your own hands then you're the same as an outlaw." Kate was pleading with the others, but she could see it was not doing any good.

Billy struggled against the rope that tied his hands. Judging from the talk, he knew that he soon would be swinging from the branch of the cottonwood.

"I say we string him up," said Mike, the Irishman.

"We do it for Mister Patrick," added Fergie.

Kate made another effort. "But Billy didn't kill Patrick. He wasn't even there and ... and he's so young."

Chisholm brushed off the argument. "It makes no difference. His partner killed him, and he's just as guilty."

Jamie had been listening quietly as he stared into the fire. He hated Billy. Chisholm was right. Billy was an outlaw. He had to be punished but a hanging without a trial? He wasn't sure.

"What about the drive?" Josh suddenly asked.

"What about it?" said Chisholm.

"Do we carry on north, up into Canada, or do we turn around and go back?"

"I say we go back," replied Chisholm. "There ain't no point in goin' further. None of us know nothin' about Canada."

"We do," said Jamie, finally breaking his silence.

"But you're just a boy. What do you know?"

"Jamie knows lots," replied Kate, defending her brother.

"Boy's don't know nothin' about the hardships of the trail. We'll be goin' though Indian country. Blackfoot country. It's said they'll lift a man's scalp just for the guns that he carries."

"Patrick said that they're peaceful," Jamie argued.

"The only reason I agreed to go on this cattle drive was because of Mister Patrick," replied Chisholm. "He knew the Blackfoot, and they knew him. He could get us across Blackfoot land and still have our hair in place."

Jamie felt panicked. Everything could be lost if he did not win this argument. "We can still get across their land."

Chisholm was on the attack. "How? You can't do it. You're just a boy!"

"But we've got to get the herd to Canada." Jamie was pleading with them now. "The people there need the cattle. Friends gave Patrick money to buy the herd. They're counting on these animals to feed them through the winter. And Conrad Kohrs gave him an advance so he could pay for the herd. We've got to get to Canada to pay them all back."

"Who would you sell the cattle to, boy? Are you a businessman? Will you get a fair price for them steers? It ain't gonna work, boy. It ain't gonna work."

Jamie was desperate now. "Patrick said that if we can just get the cattle to Canada they would fetch a good price."

"*He* might have been able to get a good price, but a boy? And how do you plan to get past the Blackfoot? You ain't a member of the North West Mounted Police. They ain't gonna listen to you. Why, I'd lay odds you don't even know none of them Blackfoot."

"Well no ..."

"What'd I tell you?"

"But we can talk to them. They're reasonable people."

Chisholm laughed. "Reasonable? I ain't never seen an Indian who was reasonable."

Jamie had the sinking feeling that he had already lost the argument but still he tried. "That's not what any Canadian would say."

"Here in the United States we know that you can never trust them people."

"That's just not true, Chisholm," said Kate. "The trouble is that here people steal their land, and then the army comes in and there is shooting."

"Well, I ain't goin' across Blackfoot land unless I'm with someone who knows them people and can get us safe passage. I say that we have a little necktie party for Billy here, and then we take this here herd back to Kohrs' Ranch."

Chisholm got to his feet, and the others followed him. The Texan had become the leader of the cowboys and their spokesman. It seemed that they would agree with anything that he proposed.

Jamie was desperate. If they took the cattle back to Kohrs' Ranch then all of Patrick's dreams would be shattered.

The whole trip would be a useless exercise. His death would be meaningless. He tried to reason with them one last time.

"If you take the cattle back to Kohrs' Ranch no one will be paid."

That seemed to catch the cowboys by surprise. "Why not?" Mike asked.

"Why would Conrad Kohrs pay you? He wasn't the one who hired you, and there are several head missing from the herd."

"But at least he's getting his animals back," argued Chisholm.

"If you help me bring the herd to Canada you'll get your pay in full." Jamie was on his feet now. He felt a new determination to see this thing through.

"You're just a boy. You ain't old enough to take this herd up to Canada."

"I can do it. I know exactly what Patrick was planning."

Chisholm shook his head. "You ain't no trail boss."

"I can do it with your help." Jamie looked desperately from man to man. "We can work together. You can help me."

But the men let Chisholm speak for them. "We're gonna finish our business with this outlaw here, and then we're gonna take these cattle back to Kohrs' Ranch."

There seemed to be nothing more to be said. One of the cowboys got his lariat. In a moment he had fixed it into a noose.

Desperately Billy struggled against the ropes. Fear and panic were etched into the boy's face. Now he knew that he was about to die.

The rope with the noose was thrown over a low-hanging branch of the cottonwood tree. Billy was untied from the chuck wagon, and his hands tied behind his back. Then two men lifted him onto the back of a pony.

Kate shrieked as they put the noose around his neck. "No! It's not right," she shouted. "He should be taken to a trial, not hung like this."

Chisholm gave his reasons again. "He's an outlaw. A rustler. That alone deserves a hangin'. But he was involved in the killin' of Mister Patrick. We're doin' this for our trail boss."

"No Chisholm! It's not fair. How can you be his judge?"

Billy was under the tree now, sitting on the horse's back, the noose tight around his throat. All it would take was to hit the horse, drive it out from under the boy, and he would strangle to death. Billy had said nothing to defend himself, nothing to explain his actions, but the terror on his face said more than any argument. At that moment all hope was gone.

"We're doin' this for our trail boss," repeated Chisholm in a loud voice so there could be no misunderstanding. "This is justice for the killin' of Mister Patrick."

Suddenly the rifle in Jamie's hand exploded into the air. He worked the pump action to move the next bullet into the chamber, and pointed the barrel at Chisholm. "There'll be no hanging today," the boy said calmly.

"He deserves to die!" one of the cowboys repeated.

"It's not what Patrick would have wanted." Jamie tried cold logic, but he did not lower the barrel of his gun. "He was a policeman. Remember? Patrick believed in the rule of law, not in vigilante justice. He would want Billy taken to trial, not hung by a mob."

The cowboys were silent. When he was alive Patrick had talked to them all about his beliefs in the importance of the law. They knew that Jamie was telling the truth.

"Take him down," Jamie continued. "We are going to take him to Canada, and Billy will go before the Queen's Magistrate once we get there."

"What about the cattle?" asked Chisholm angrily.

"The cattle were bought and paid for fair and square by Patrick. He wanted to take them to Canada, and that's what we're going to do."

"We can't do that!" shouted the Texan.

"Every man who comes with us to Canada will get his full pay when we get there. That's a promise. Anyone who doesn't want to continue the drive can leave now."

There was a deadly silence among the men. They could tell from the look on the boy's face that he was determined to carry out his words.

Finally it was Josh that broke the silence. "I'll come with you, Mister Jamie."

The others looked at the big man. Josh was liked and respected by the crew, but he was a black man, and that made them uncertain of his authority.

But Jamie had no doubts. "Good, Josh, and I'll take any other man who's willing to come with us, but we're going to Canada. That's a promise, and they'll be no hanging today. Now take Billy down."

A moment later the outlaw was on the ground. His wrists were still firmly tied together, but the noose was taken from around his neck.

11

That afternoon the cowboys talked endlessly as each of them considered what they were going to do. Jamie waited for them to make up their minds. He knew that there was not much more he could say or do to convince them to continue the cattle drive.

Jamie found a moment to thank Josh. The vote of confidence of one of the best cowboys in the outfit made the continuation of the drive a real possibility. But when Jamie spoke to him, the big cowboy simply put his hand on his shoulder and said nothing. They both knew that they would have to recruit others, or they would have a hard time moving the cattle north.

After Josh, Trapper was the next one to say that he was willing to continue the drive. He needed the money, he told Jamie. Trapper was a loner who made up his own mind about things. The others still looked to Chisholm for leadership.

Once, late in the afternoon, Jamie passed by Billy, still tied to the chuck wagon, and the outlaw tried his best to thank the person who had saved his life, but Jamie brushed by him without a word. He wanted nothing to do with this bandit who had contributed to the death of his friend. The magistrate in Canada would deal with him, and Jamie hoped that he would be punished with the full measure of the law.

Chisholm brooded alone. He was not the type of man who took kindly to being bested by a fifteen-year-old boy. Others came up to talk to him, but he shrugged them off and said little to anyone.

Over supper Jamie stated his position again so everyone around the fire would understand him. "Tomorrow at sunup the drive begins again. Kate, Josh, Trapper and I are taking the cattle to Canada. Any other man who wants to join us is welcome. You'll get your full pay when I sell the steers."

"The four of you can't handle the herd," said Chisholm, bitterly.

"We're leaving in the morning," Jamie repeated in a determined way. "You're welcome to join us, Chisholm."

Nothing more was said. The cowboys talked to each other in tight little circles, but no one said a word to Jamie.

The sunset was spreading its gold and red colours in the western sky when Josh sat beside Jamie. "What do you think they're gonna do?" the big cowboy asked quietly.

"I don't know, but the men are still riding their watch on the herd. That means they haven't quit yet," Jamie whispered in reply.

Josh nodded. "It'll be up to Chisholm."

"He's still angry that I stopped the lynching."

"You done good to stop the lynchin', Mister Jamie. My people suffer from that way of thinkin'." The black man was quiet for a long moment, and then he asked, "You want me to talk to Chisholm?"

"No. He'll make his own mind up in time."

In the middle of the night Jamie and Josh rode their watch on the herd. All was quiet. The stars gleamed overhead in a cloudless sky, and a half-moon cast a pale light across the barren landscape. The cattle grazed and rested.

Jamie was worried. Never before had he taken on anything like this. To become the trail boss on a cattle drive through unknown territory with hostile Indians was hard enough for a boy, but if he had to set out with only half a crew it might be impossible. Maybe Chisholm was right, and he should give up and return the herd to Kohrs' Ranch.

But no. He was determined to take the cattle north. He owed it to Patrick to try and realize his dream, and the people in Canada needed the cattle. But how was he going to convince the cowboys that he could do it? That was the thing. They had to believe in him, just as they had believed in Patrick. The boy climbed into his bedroll after his watch with nothing resolved.

Before dawn Jamie was up. Lee had made a big breakfast, and the cowboys ate in a hurry. The boy glanced at his sister. She was smiling at him, but still he did not know what the crew was going to do. He saddled his stallion. The rest of the men were saddling up as well, including Chisholm.

Jamie rode to the front of the herd. Lee was ready with the chuck wagon, with the prisoner tied to the seat beside him. Every cowboy in the outfit had moved into position. Even Chisholm was there, riding at left point. The boy felt a surge of excitement. The cowboys were going to go with them!

"Take 'em out, Mister Jamie!" Josh shouted and then laughed.

"Ho cattle, ho, ho, ho!" the boy called to his crew. The cry was repeated from man to man. "Ho cattle, ho!" "Ho cattle!" Slowly the cowboys began moving the herd north towards Canada.

The routine of the trail soon returned. They drove the herd easily in the morning, making a couple of miles, and then stopped for dinner about noon. After the break they pushed the herd harder, making ten or possibly twelve miles before they stopped for the night to let the cattle graze.

Everyone in the outfit took up their same chores with two exceptions. Kate was made the wrangler, herding the horses, and Jamie was the trail boss. He was responsible for every detail of the drive. The trail boss had to find the route to follow, and in uninhabited country, that could be difficult. He had to look after the crew and find good pastures and water for the herd. It was not easy.

Every morning, once the drive was underway, Jamie rode ahead to scout out the best trail. He had Patrick's map, which was helpful, but it lacked details and was often inaccurate. The mountains were barely sketched in, and what appeared on the map to be a gentle stream could turn out to be a raging river, or a river could turn out to be a stream.

For hours, Jamie poured over that map. Patrick had drawn a line in pencil marking what he thought would be the best route, but the more the boy understood the limitations of the map, and the nature of the country, the more he knew that line was no more than a rough approximation.

"Do you know where you're taking us?" Kate asked one evening as they sat in the glow of the fire. But Jamie was so absorbed in his map that he did not even hear her.

"Leave him," Josh said softly. "He'll find the way."

"He'd better. Everything depends on him."

Jamie quickly learned that the easiest thing to find was good grazing land and water. Many streams came out of the mountains, to the west of them, and there were rich pastures almost everywhere. The real challenge was finding the best way north. In one sense it was easy. All they had to do was keep the mountains, to the west, within sight and head due north. In time they would come into Canada.

The problem was there were no trails. They had come to the southern edge of what was considered Blackfoot land. No settlers or ranchers lived there. A few trappers and prospectors came into the area, and the U.S. Army sent out patrols, but there were no established trails other than the ones used by the Indians. The new trail boss had to choose his own trail.

Jamie learned that he had to be constantly on the move. He would ride a long way ahead scouting out the best route. He knew he had to avoid high hills that would exhaust the herd, and he had to be careful that he did not lead the cattle over a cliff, but it was the rivers that gave the most trouble. Often when he came across a rapid stream blocking their way north he had to ride upriver for a distance until he found an easy place to cross. Once he found a good fording spot he would then have to ride back to the herd to redirect the cowboys.

More than once on those first days when he became trail boss Jamie found signs of native people. Once he came across the remains of a teepee circle on a plateau overlooking a river valley. The boy studied the scorched ground of the fires and decided that the site had not been used for three or possibly four years. On a fast-flowing river he found the ford marked by feathers tied to branches of trees. But nowhere did he see Blackfoot people. The young trail boss never told the cowboys about seeing the signs. The last thing that he wanted was for them to get panicked about the possibility of an attack.

Jamie changed in those first days when he became trail boss. He became quiet and watchful. The responsibility worried him. He knew that the men had to trust and respect him if they were going to continue the drive up into the Canadian foothills country. If they had the sense that he did not know what he was doing, or was frightened, they would lose confidence in him. That could lead to disaster.

Chisholm was hardest to understand or predict. The Texan did his job as well as ever, and he was still one of the best cowboys in the outfit, but he talked little to Jamie or Josh or any of the others. It was like he was waiting for Jamie to make a blunder so that he could demonstrate that he had been right all along, and they must abandon the cattle drive.

But every day the herd covered another ten or twelve miles. Slowly they were making their way north. Gradually the cowboys came to accept the new order. "Mister Jamie," came to be the new name used by the cowboys for their trail boss, and the new wrangler came to be known as "Miss Kate." Jamie smiled to himself when he heard these names. Both he and his sister had risen in status from the days when they were simply called "boy" and "girl."

But Jamie knew that the cowboys had not accepted them completely. The drive was going through easy country, where men and cattle could look after themselves. What would happen if things got tough?

Kate liked her job as wrangler. She was up on her horse from morning to night, but it was work she enjoyed. The horses had accepted the routine. They were still half-wild, and she had to be careful when she was around them, but they knew what was expected of them, and they were herded easily.

The one thing that did bother her was that she was still expected to help Lee, the cook, at meal times. It meant that she was working from before the sun broke the horizon in the morning until long after supper. She had to knead the dough for the biscuits, fetch water from nearby streams, make coffee and wash the mountain of pots, pans and dishes that were created every meal. It wasn't fair, Kate thought. She had more than enough to do just looking after the horses.

"Jamie," she said to her brother one evening after supper. "I need some help with the camp chores."

"I don't have time, Kate. You've got to do it yourself." And he went back to his map.

But there was the prisoner. Kate looked up to see Billy tied to the wheel of the chuck wagon, not contributing a thing. Why couldn't he do a little work to pay for his keep?

What a sad and sorry sight Billy was. No one had paid any attention to him since that fateful day when he was almost lynched. The cowboys sometimes cussed him; one even made like he was going to spit on him to show his disgust. The boy was so downcast and defeated that Kate wondered if he would have the energy to work. Maybe he would be more of a nuisance than a help.

One evening as she began to wash the dishes in a big tub that she had set close to the prisoner, she said to him, "Are you just going to sit there and do nothing the rest of the drive, Billy."

"What else can I do?" he replied as downcast as ever.

"You weren't always so easy to get along with."

"I'm tied up all the time, Kate. What can I do?"

"Would you help me wash the dishes?" The girl's arms were into soapy water up to her elbows.

"They won't take off these ropes. They just want to see me hung."

"You can't blame them, Billy."

"But I didn't kill Patrick. You've got to believe me." He was close to tears.

"Save it for the judge."

"Your brother won't even talk to me. I ain't even had a chance to explain."

Kate went back to washing the dishes. What could she say to Billy that would make any difference? Jamie had saved him from the lynch mob, but Billy would have to face a judge in Canada, and he might still be hung for his crimes. But she was curious.

"Why did you become an outlaw, anyway?" she asked.

The boy shrugged. He was sitting on the ground, his feet and hands tied to a wheel of the chuck wagon, his head sunk between his knees. "It's a long story," he murmured.

"It looks like we will have a long time on this cattle drive. You might as well tell me."

Billy looked up at the darkening sky. Voices of the cowboys relaxing around the campfire drifted over to them. Jamie was studying the map intently.

"I was born on a farm in Missouri. Dirt poor. My ma had eight babies, most died. Then she died. My pa had nothin' … nothin' but a couple o' pigs and a cow and some corn. So one day he came home with another woman and there weren't no place for me so I up and left."

"How old were you?"

"Twelve."

"You didn't say goodbye or anything?" Kate and Jamie came from a close family that tried to look after each other. She found it hard to imagine a twelve-year-old being forced out of his home.

Billy nodded. "Just walked out one day and never looked back."

"What did you do then?"

"Drifted west. I worked in a livery stable for a time, but the man didn't like me much. I quit and headed out. Walked a long way. I don't know where. Some people gave me things to eat. Sometimes I stole just to get food to stay alive. A few times they throwed me in jail. Jail wasn't bad. At least I got somethin' to eat."

Billy was into the flow of his story, and Kate did not have to prompt him any more. "I hooked up with a wagon train headin' west with some settlers. Nice people, they were. They fed me, and I drove a wagon pulled by a pair of oxen. Out in the Dakotas somewheres we was attacked by Sioux. Some got killed. I barely got away with my scalp. Then I worked in mining camps in Colorado and Montana. It was there that I met up with McCoy."

"Was he always as bad as when we knew him?"

"He was good to me. At least after I teamed up with him I never went hungry. He got me stuff: a horse, an outfit, guns."

"And then you went into crime with him," Kate added.

"Yeah, well. It was all we knew." Billy grew silent. He stirred the dust at his feet.

It was a sad story, Kate thought, but it didn't excuse the murder of Patrick, and the lives they led as outlaws. "Do you miss him?"

Billy looked up at her as if trying to judge what answer she was looking for, but he told the simple truth. "Yes, maybe. There was a wildness about McCoy that wouldn't let him rest. He always had to be doin' things and gettin' into trouble, but we were partners. We looked after each other. I never had that before."

"But he got you into trouble. Deep trouble."

The boy put his hands to his face as if to cover his fear. "And now I'm gonna pay for it. Once we get up to Canada they're gonna try me for murder. I won't have a chance. They already ordered me out of the country once. Now they're gonna say I helped kill a policeman. What chance do you think I have? What's the difference between bein' hung by a magistrate's order or hung by a lynch mob? You're dead just the same." Tears were flowing down Billy's face as he finished. The boy stirred the dust and was silent.

The darkness had gathered. The cowboys joked and told stories around the campfire. Jamie was at work trying to find the best route to Canada. The men on watch sang to the cattle under the star-filled sky. Every one of them had friends and a place in the world. Billy faced a bleak future alone, without anyone to support him.

"If I can get Jamie to agree, will you help me around the camp, Billy?" Kate asked softly.

"Help you? Yes. I'd like that Kate," and for the first time Billy smiled.

Kate talked to her brother about getting Billy to help around the camp. At first he did not want anything to do with it.

"He's an outlaw, Kate, a murderer. I won't have him as part of the outfit."

"But I've got too much to do, Jamie. I can't look after the horses and wash all those dishes and help with the cooking. It's too much. I'm working harder than anyone on the drive."

"I won't have Billy," Jamie repeated stubbornly.

Kate was furious. "You've become a little dictator since you became trail boss, Jamie Bains! It's not fair!" And she stomped away from her brother in anger.

Jamie gave up. He could face a lot of problems on this cattle drive, but having his sister mad at him was one thing he did not need. The trail boss spoke to Josh, and that night the cowboy fashioned a new type of binding where Billy's hands were free, but his legs were still hobbled so he could not get away.

Lee was not very happy when he learned who his new helper was going to be, but by the next morning Billy was helping to prepare the food and washing the pots and dishes that were created. In a day or so the cook had to concede that his new "cook's help" was a pretty good worker.

Billy was different than he had been before. He had lost that swaggering hostility and was quiet, even cautious and polite.

As the drive continued north towards Canada they were getting deeper into Blackfoot country. Jamie worried about how they would be received, but it was the rivers that posed the most immediate problem. The streams were high at that time of the year, and the water, which came from melted snow up in the mountains, was frigid cold.

The map showed a big river that they would have to cross, and as they got close Jamie rode on ahead to find it. They were in rolling foothills country. To the west they could see the Rocky Mountain range, running like a spine on a north-south axis. Their trail took them through open grasslands covered with "prairie wool," as he had heard cowboys call it. It was rich range land that had sustained the buffalo for thousands of years.

Riding alone through that country gave the boy a feeling of freedom. Often he came across elk, mule deer and antelope grazing. Wolves lurked well out of range, watching and waiting. Badgers, and gophers ran from the hooves of his horse. There were magpies, hawks, eagles and a number of other birds he did not recognize. It was a country that made him feel alive with possibilities but still anxious about the dangers. As he watched the land and wildlife he looked for any sign of the Blackfoot.

He was a good ways ahead of the herd when he finally came across the river. Jamie stopped by its bank and watched the water as it tumbled over rocks and swept past him. The river was fifty yards wide, but in the centre the deep, powerful current bubbled and surged in a dangerous, threatening way.

Jamie rode west along the bank for a couple of miles looking for the best place to cross, but the land rose up into a series of hills. In the distance the hills turned into the cliffs and rocky crags of the mountains. The deep gorge cut by the river made it impossible for the cattle to get down to the water.

The trail boss turned around and rode in the other direction. Downstream a distance the river broadened out. The banks were lower making it easier for the cattle to get to the water's edge, but the river was fast and treacherous. Finally he picked the best spot to cross. He marked it by tying a piece of cloth that he carried onto a scrub brush, and then turned back towards the herd.

This would be a hard crossing, he knew that, but there was no alternative. As he rode Jamie tried to think of what he could do to reduce the risks. Chisholm was his best hope. The Texan had more experience crossing rivers than anyone else in the outfit, but he was still nursing the bruising he received and was barely talking to Jamie, or anyone else for that matter.

The boy found the outfit about five miles back of the river as the cowboys were bedding down the herd for the night. When things had settled, and the men were drinking their coffee after supper, Jamie described the river they would have to cross the next day.

"What do you think, Chisholm?" he asked in an effort to draw out the Texan.

"River crossin's always the worst part of the drive. I seen a hundred head o' cattle drowned on one crossin' on the Chisholm Trail. Terrible sight. Dead carcasses everywhere."

"What's the real danger?"

"Some o' them cattle can swim just like swans, but the water panics others. They get out in the middle of the river where they're swimming, and then for no reason one or two will turn around and head back for the shore they left. Then the whole herd starts millin' about, hitting each other with their hooves and horns. They get swept down river. It's a terrible thing to see."

"What can we do to prevent that?" Jamie asked.

Chisholm was talking more than he had for days. "You've got to get 'em movin'. The herd should reach the river almost at a dead run. And you've got to keep that pace so they sweep across the river and up the bank on the other side. If they panic and turn back it'll be a disaster."

"That's a tall order," one of the men commented.

"And what if they do try and turn back?" Josh asked.

"That's when it gets hard. You've got to rope the leader and pull him across. Get the herd moving again so that the cattle comin' behind keep followin' the one in front of them."

"Does that mean we gotta be in the water, Mister Jamie?" Buck asked.

"Looks like it."

"Well, I don't swim none. I'm scared o' the water."

"I don't even like to wash in water," added Mike, with his usual Irish humour. "Sure as you're not gonna get me in there."

"I can do it," said Billy suddenly. He had been listening as he washed the dishes. "I grew up swimming in the Mississippi River. I'm not afraid of water."

But the cowboys would have nothing to do with the outlaw. As far as they were concerned Billy was not part of the outfit. They did not even want to talk to him.

The crew discussed the river crossing for a long time. Jamie let Chisholm take the leadership. He knew more about river crossings than anyone else in the outfit, certainly more than their new trail boss, and Jamie saw that this was a way to bring him back and involve him in the cattle drive. He needed the Texan and his experience.

The next morning they got the herd moving early and drove them to within a half a mile of the crossing that Jamie had marked. They let the herd graze, and Jamie led a group of the cowboys on ahead to look at the river.

Chisholm watched the water and talked about the risks. "That water's mighty fast and cold. We've got to keep them cattle movin' or we could be in for some real trouble."

Lee and Billy were riding up on the chuck wagon. Jamie and the others rode over to them. "I want you to take the wagon across first, Lee," he told the cook.

"You sure it's safe, Mister Jamie?"

"You can do it, Lee. Just don't let those horses turn. Away you go."

"You've got to untie me," Billy called out to him. "If the chuck wagon is swept downstream then I can swim for it."

For a moment the trail boss was tempted to say no. It would serve Billy right, but he could not do it. "If you take this chance to escape, Billy, I promise I'll hunt you down." The look on Jamie's face showed he was dead serious. "Untie him, Lee, but don't let him out of your sight. Now get your wagon moving."

Billy had saddled his own horse that morning, and it trailed behind the chuck wagon as they took it across the river. Jamie and the group of cowboys watched from the shore as the wagon went across. It was an unsettling sight.

They were only a few yards into the river when the bottom disappeared, and the horses had to swim. The wagon floated but water came rushing in, soaking nearly everything. Lee was having trouble managing the team. One horse panicked and fought to turn around. The other animals were confused and began to thrash about. The wagon was caught in the current and started to sweep downstream.

Billy took the reins from Lee's hands and beat the backs of the horses with them, shouting: "Hi up! Git up, there! Hi up! ... Hi up!" He cracked the whip over their heads. The four animals began to respond by swimming for the other shore.

Once they were out in the centre of the river the current swept them downstream all the faster. All they could see was the horses' heads. Water was up to the floorboards of the wagon, but still Billy called out to the team, and still they responded by swimming hard for the other shore. Finally the two lead horses hit the gravel bottom, and a moment later the four horses were pulling the wagon up onto the opposite bank. Lee was panic-struck, but he managed to put his hand on Billy's shoulder and thank him.

Back on the other side of the river the cowboys were even more worried now that they had seen the trouble the chuck wagon had gotten into. "What do you think, Chisholm?" Jamie asked.

"The current's mighty strong. I dunno. Maybe we should try and find a better place to cross."

Jamie surveyed the scene. He had been up river, and there was no crossing there. Down river looked no better. They couldn't afford to go hundreds of miles out of their way. The decision was his, and he made it. "We cross here, and we're gonna do it now. You take them across, Chisholm. You're in command."

The Texan nodded, and the men rode back to the herd. He gathered the cowboys together and gave them instructions. "Keep the critters movin'. By the time they hit the river I want them almost in a run. Don't let them double back what-ever happens. Mister Jamie, you stay out in front. The leaders of the herd will follow you and your horse so don't turn back. Ride straight across to the other side."

The men were in position. Kate was with the horses towards the back of the herd. Jamie was at the front. The boy looked back at Chisholm, and the cowboy gave a nod.

"Cattle ho! Ho cattle, ho!" the trail boss shouted and the call was repeated from man to man. The herd was beginning to move. The cowboys pressed them hard. The cattle sensed that something special was happening. They formed into a line, going at a fast walk. Some broke into a run.

Jamie, out in front, moved his stallion into an easy trot. Looking back, he saw that the lead steers were following him close behind, and the rest of the herd, strung out four or five abreast, were moving with them at the same pace. The earth was shaking with the pounding of hooves.

The trail boss led the herd from the prairie, down the riverbank and into the water, thundering forward like a powerful rolling wave. They were almost at a run when they hit the water. The cattle did not know what was happening until they were into the cold river. Then they bellowed and mooed, but still they moved forward, pressed on by those behind and by the sheer momentum of the herd.

Jamie stayed out in front. His horse was swimming now and behind him the lead steers were swimming as well. He felt the frigid water surge up to his waist. The current tugged at them and began to sweep them downstream, but his stallion kept moving forward with the strokes of his powerful legs.

They were three quarters of the way across the river; most of the herd was in the water, and the horses, driven by Kate, had almost reached the water's edge, when panic struck. It started with only one steer who lost his bearings, turned and began heading back the way they had come. Others joined the panic and in a moment the front of the herd was a milling, frightened mob flailing with their sharp hooves in all directions.

Jamie was out in front. He could see what was happening, but he could do nothing about it. Chisholm and Josh, riding point, not far behind, shouted at the panicking animals, hitting their rumps with the ends of their lariats. They had to get them moving again or it would be a disaster.

Suddenly Billy was in the water aboard his pony. He swung his lariat about his head, and in one deft throw snagged the horns of the steer causing the panic. In a moment he had turned his horse and fought for the other side. Billy's horse hit gravel and heaved up into shallow water, the rope around the steer grew taut. The animal was being dragged towards shore by Billy's pony. Other cattle saw the movement and began to follow. It took a minute to get the momentum of the drive re-established, but when it happened the herd flowed forward again in one continuous wave until they hit the gravel bottom. Chisholm and Josh were there, driving the cattle up the bank and over to the pasture on the other side.

The herd was moving well now, but towards the end, where the cows and calves ran, there was more trouble. Two of the youngest calves were swept away downstream. Their mothers turned and swam after them. The cowboys, Buck and Trapper, were too frightened of the water to follow them.

Billy saw what was happening and raced with his pony along the river bank. He got downstream from the calves and then plunged into the water. His pony swam hard until the boy was beside the terrified calves. Quickly he slipped the noose of his lariat over the heads of both calves and then his horse swam for shore. In a moment the hooves of his pony had hit bottom, and he hauled the two calves, squealing with fright, out onto dry ground. Behind them one of the cows managed to swim after them, but the other was swept downstream and was lost.

Billy was riding back, leading the two calves and the cow, just as Kate was driving the last of the horses up the bank. The herd of cattle was grazing contentedly on the other side of the river. Jamie and the rest of the outfit were resting beside the chuck wagon, congratulating themselves on getting across safely.

It was Chisholm who recognized what the outlaw had done to save the herd. "You done well, boy," he said simply, and then he walked away. Jamie stared hard at Billy but said nothing.

But they hardly took a moment to rest before they were heading north again. The next day the trail boss was a mile in front of the herd scouting out the best route when he saw two Blackfoot on a hill in the distance watching him. For the first time Jamie felt uneasy and rode back to the safety of the others. When they brought the herd up the Blackfoot were still watching.

"It ain't good," Chisholm commented when they stopped for the noon meal. "They got rifles. We wouldn't have a chance against them."

"Buffalo are scarce," Buck added. "They've got to be mighty hungry."

"Yeah," said another cowboy. "Our herd will look good to them."

"Hunger drives a man to action faster than anythin' else," concluded Chisholm.

"What are we gonna do, Mister Jamie?" Fergie asked.

"We've been heading north all this time. We're not turning around now."

"Wish we had a few more men," said Chisholm. "That way we could fight 'em off."

Billy had been listening closely. "I could help," he said.

Josh nodded. "The boy helped us a lot at the river crossin'."

"No!" said Jamie firmly. "Billy's a prisoner. He's going to trial as soon as we get to Canada. He's not to have any weapons."

Jamie got to his feet and walked out towards the hills to look for any signs of Blackfoot. He was nervous, though he would admit it to no one. The Blackfoot did not like strangers coming onto their land. Buck was right, with the passing of the buffalo they would be hungry, and the fat cattle in their herd were a real temptation.

But the trail boss insisted that they keep to their routine. The next day they drove another ten miles north. They were going deeper and deeper into Blackfoot territory towards the foothills country of Canada. There was no turning back now.

That day a group of ten cattle got spooked for some reason and made a break for freedom. Jamie sent a couple of cowboys out after them. He was short-handed and, against his better judgment, asked Billy if he would ride drag until they came back. The boy was happy to agree. For the first time he was riding with the outfit.

A few hours later the cowboys returned with the cattle. They had unsettling news. Once they rounded up the lost cattle, they had come across a band of Blackfoot. The natives saw them coming and took out their rifles and bows and arrows. It looked for a moment like they might attack, but then the Blackfoot let them pass.

"Somethin's happenin' out there," said Chisholm. "It's likely they've been watchin' us for days now, just waitin' for the right moment to attack."

"I don't like it," added another cowboy.

Kate felt the nervousness and talked to Jamie when the two were alone. "The cowboys expect an attack. They're fixing their guns. What are you going to do?"

On the outside Jamie was perfectly calm. "We're going to go north, right through Blackfoot country." He said the same thing to every other member of the outfit who asked, but inside he was in turmoil. Had they gone too far? Would the Blackfoot attack? Should they turn back before it's too late? He just did not know.

Late the same afternoon a group of twenty Blackfoot suddenly appeared. Jamie felt panic in the pit of his stomach. They were all heavily armed warriors with rifles, bows and long spears, riding their war ponies. Most had spotted horses decorated with paint, and some had their faces painted to make them appear frightening to their enemies.

Nervously the cowboys loosened their weapons. Most rode with their rifles in front of them across their saddles, ready for action. Jamie knew he had to head off trouble before it started, and he rode from man to man telling them to put away their weapons. "If the Blackfoot think we are going to attack they'll be onto us in a moment. We won't have a chance." Reluctantly the cowboys followed the order.

Without a word the Blackfoot rode down on either side of the herd as if they were on an inspection. Then, as soon as they had surveyed the herd, they galloped away in the direction they had come. No one on either side had said a word.

13

Jamie insisted that they continue the drive in the usual manner until supper time. The others were nervous.

Buck came riding up to him. "Mister Jamie, we've got to stop now and make our defenses before they attack!"

"Now is not the time to lose our nerve," the trail boss replied.

"But they could attack at any moment!"

"Go back to your position, Buck. We're pressing on!"

Reluctantly the cowboy did as he was told. But Jamie was not sure he was doing the right thing. Maybe the Blackfoot were getting reinforcements. They could sweep down on them and in a moment cut them to pieces.

The boy felt totally alone. Was he right in going forward? Maybe they were riding to their death, just as Custer and his men had met their death the summer before. Maybe the Blackfoot were so hungry that they would kill them all just to take the cattle.

But no, they had to carry on. They would be vastly outnumbered and could never defend themselves or the cattle, but even if they turned around they could be attacked. All they could do was go forward.

For another two hours they rode north, driving the cattle farther and farther into Blackfoot country. Jamie only called a halt to the drive at supper, the same time as they stopped every evening.

The routine was the same. Lee and Billy had the supper of beans, salt pork and biscuits ready with strong coffee boiling over the fire; Kate drove the horses into a rope corral so the cowboys could pick out the mounts they would use for their turn on night watch; and the members of the outfit gathered around the fire for their supper, while others rode guard on the herd. Nothing had changed except the sense of nervous fear among the crew.

Jamie studied the hills that rose up to the west of them. He searched long and hard. There was not a sign of the Blackfoot, but he knew that they were out there somewhere, watching them.

"What do you think, Mister Jamie?" Mike asked.

"I dunno."

Buck was agitated. "They're gettin' ready to lift our scalps, if you ask me."

"I don't think so," said the trail boss.

"You can just feel it in the air. They're out there in them hills, and they're gonna pounce at any moment. Maybe they'll attack tonight."

"If that's what they plan they would have done it already."

Buck was not satisfied. "Well I don't like the idea of sittin' here waitin' for them Indians to butcher us."

"Me neither, Buck," Fergie added. "I seen the work of them Indians, and it ain't pretty." Fergie was not a man who often gave his opinion.

"Look," Jamie said slowly so they could all consider his words. "The Blackfoot have been peaceful. In Canada, the North West Mounted Police have helped them and are respected by them. We're going to Canada, and this drive has been organized by Canadians. We've got to think that they will look kindly on us. If we start shooting at them or start building defenses then they'll see us as hostile and attack for sure. We'll lose the cattle, and maybe our lives."

"The trail boss is right," said Josh.

"We just carry on," Jamie continued, "like nothing different has happened."

But the speech upset Buck. "What do you know, Mister Jamie? Or you, Josh? You ever had dealin' with them Blackfoot? I heard tell that the Blackfoot will kill you as soon as look at you. All them Indians are the same."

"Up in Canada Indian people are our partners, not enemies," said Kate.

"You sure it's any better in Canada?" asked Chisholm.

"At least we're not driving them off the land."

"Not yet maybe," added the Texan.

"Look, I don't like this here situation one bit," said Buck. "They ain't gonna see us as friends. We're crossin' their land, and they're not gonna be happy about that. If we were led by Mister Patrick it might be different. The Blackfoot knew him, but if you ask me they are just waitin' for us, and our hair is gonna be flyin' on one of their coup sticks if we keep tryin' to go north across their land."

"Yer right, Buck," agreed Fergie.

"Well I ain't goin' any farther. They ain't gonna get old Bucko here. No sir."

"What are you gonna do, Buck?" Josh asked.

"Tomorrow mornin' I'm headin' out of here. Goin' south. They ain't gonna get my pretty lock of hair fer decoration."

Fergie was nodding. "I'm with you, Buck."

"That's foolish," said Jamie. He knew he had to head off this rebellion or he could be left with no crew at all. "It's best to stay together. Men alone will be targets."

But Buck was determined. "We'll be headin' away from Blackfoot land. Don't you see? The herd and the rest of you'se will be aimin' to head right through their land. That'll make 'em upset."

Jamie knew that he had to appear confident. "If you want to go, Buck, there is nothing I can do to stop you, but you know that I don't have the money to pay you your wages. The only ones who will be paid are those who ride all the way to Canada."

Buck laughed. "Money or your life. Some choice. I'm gonna take my life. I'm headin' out tomorrow. Are you comin' with me, Fergie?"

"You bet I am. These Blackfoot ain't gonna get me."

Jamie was on his feet. "Well I say you're making a mistake, but every man has to decide for himself. Tomorrow morning this herd is heading north towards Canada and nothing is gonna stop us."

He walked away from the fire. He had had enough of this pessimistic talk. If anything, the discussion had made him more determined. There was no turning back now. It was not a matter of being brave or a coward. They would either meet the Blackfoot when they went farther north, or they would meet them on the way south. One way or another they had to deal with them.

"You done the right thing, Mister Jamie."

He whirled around. It was Billy, the last person in the world he wanted to talk to.

But the boy outlaw continued. "I just wanted you to know that I'm with you, and I'll do what I can to help."

Jamie looked at him long and hard. The sincerity on Billy's face seemed genuine. "Thank you, Billy," he found himself saying, even though he still had a deep distrust of the outlaw.

For much of that evening Buck held forth on his reasons for abandoning the cattle drive while Fergie, sitting beside him, agreed with his every word. Later Buck asked others their opinion.

"What about you, Josh? Are you foolish enough to carry on?"

The southern man smiled in the easy way that he had. "The trail boss, and Miss Kate, they're special people. Real leaders. I reckon I'm gonna stay with them to the end."

"What about you, Chisholm?" Buck asked.

"I figure I want to see my pay at the end of the trail."

Jamie felt a huge sense of relief to hear those words. The others were quiet but he knew he had their support.

With the coming of darkness, Jamie posted three men to ride watch on the herd, rather than the usual two. If an attack came at least they would have a small chance to mount a defense. But it was a quiet night. The moon drifted in a cloudless sky. Wolves howled from the hills, and the cattle grazed and rested like there was nothing special about to happen.

Jamie felt lonelier than at any time in his life. What if he was wrong? What if the Blackfoot were waiting until they got deep into their territory before they sprang an ambush. Was he leading his crew into a trap?

Despite his doubts Jamie knew he had to appear calm and confident to the cowboys. If he showed fear of any kind they could lose faith in him and panic. That was the road to disaster. It took all of his energy to maintain a look of confidence and composure. To the others he appeared utterly calm; his face was blank; he spoke little to anyone; but deep down his doubts made him shudder to the core of his being.

That night, sleeping in his bedroll, he woke up in a cold sweat, dreaming that the worst had happened, only to find calm in the camp. By morning he felt drained, but he reminded himself that he must not betray his fears to anyone, not even Kate. He got up, ate breakfast and went about camp as if everything was normal.

Buck and Fergie packed up their gear and got ready to head out. When they came to say goodbye to the trail boss, Buck was generous.

"It's not like we've got anythin' against you, Mister Jamie. You've been good to us. But a man's got to think what's good for himself."

Buck and Fergie shook hands all around, climbed onto their horses, and in a moment they were heading south, back down the trail from where they had come.

Jamie delivered his orders to the crew as they stood around the campfire. "Billy, if you're willing, I'd like you to ride drag."

"Happy to, Mister Jamie."

"Miss Kate, put the horses in with the herd. You're going to have to cover Buck's position. Lee, keep the chuck wagon in close to the herd. I don't want you going off ahead to make camp. No one wanders away from the rest of us for any reason. We have to stay close together. Agreed?"

Everyone nodded assent.

"One other thing," the trail boss said. "Keep your weapons in their holsters. A cowboy waving around a gun is an invitation to be attacked. All right, let's move 'em out."

Everyone rode to their positions. "Ho cattle, ho!" Jamie called, and the command was repeated by the others. The trail boss nudged his stallion gently and began to ride north. Slowly the herd gathered and soon they began to move at a walking pace north, into the heart of Blackfoot country.

As they rode Jamie studied the scene for signs. In the hills he could see smoke that could be coming from cooking fires. Far off in the distance to the west he thought he could see horses and riders, but he could not be sure. There was little game about. Maybe they had been frightened by something.

Less than two hours after they had started on the trail Jamie could hear a commotion behind him. He turned around only to see Buck and Fergie riding hard to catch up with them. Jamie signalled to Chisholm and Josh to settle the herd while he rode to find what the trouble was all about.

Buck was breathless. "They're all around us, Mister Jamie."

"What do you mean?"

"We rode south, and we seen at least ten warriors up in the hills. Then there was a bunch more waitin' for us on the road, so we turned around and hightailed it back here as fast as we could."

"Did they fire at you?"

"No, but they were gonna attack for sure."

"How do you know?"

"It just looked like that, Mister Jamie. That's all. They were all done up in their feathers and paint and things, and they had their rifles and their bows, and they were riding their fast war ponies. I tell you they're gettin' ready to attack. And they're gonna attack us here." Buck was in a complete panic.

"I don't see any Blackfoot," Jamie said calmly, but he could feel the fear rise within him.

"They was right on our trail. I tell you they're gonna attack. We could be gonners. We've got to turn around or do somethin'."

"You tried that, Buck. Now we're going to follow my plan."

"We'll do anything, Mister Jamie, anything. Just let us stay here with you and the herd. That way we've got some protection."

The two of them had been spooked. Normally Buck and Fergie were good cowboys, as brave as the next man, but Jamie knew that he could not rely on them, at least for the time being. "Why don't the two of you ride up with Lee on the chuck wagon. I've got the crew reorganized, and the herd is driving well. Just stay with Lee. He might need your help."

"Sure ... sure thing," said Fergie.

Buck eagerly agreed. "Anything you want us to do, Mister Jamie. Just name it, but we're gonna stay here with you now. You can bet on that."

Once they had settled in the chuck wagon Jamie rode to the front of the herd. Again he waved his arm and gave the call. The herd began to move.

A type of calm had come over Jamie. He knew the cowboys were watching him, waiting to see how he dealt with every detail. He looked back at his crew. Every one of them was concentrating on the herd. Even Kate was working well in her position of flank rider. They seemed to trust him and his judgment implicitly. He could only hope that their trust was justified.

All morning long they drove the cattle gently, as was the routine. Then about noon, Jamie saw something in the distance ahead of them. Horses. A moment later he could see that it was men on horseback. Many men. A hundred or more Blackfoot, and they were riding towards them at an easy trot. The closer they came the clearer the boy could see that they had weapons: rifles, spears and bows, with quivers full of arrows. These were warriors, the best of the Blackfoot tribe, and they had come to challenge them.

Jamie held his hand up and signalled that the cowboys were to keep the herd tight together but to let them graze. Then he rode forward a short distance and waited for the Blackfoot. Fear made the hair on the back of his neck stand up, but his face betrayed no emotion.

14

The Blackfoot warriors were dressed in full regalia. Some of the younger men were bare chested with buckskin leggings. The older men had elaborately decorated shirts, some wore breast plates, but only a few had feathers in their war bonnets and war paint.

The look and mood of the Blackfoot made Jamie feel uneasy. They were determined, impatient men, ready for action.

The trail boss waited. On either side of him were Josh and Chisholm. Then Kate joined them while the others tended the herd. The Blackfoot rode to within easy talking distance. One of the chiefs, an older man with long hair and a sharp aquiline nose, held up his hand and the warriors reined to a stop.

Jamie held up his hand in greeting and then spoke in a loud voice so everyone could hear. "We give greetings to the Blackfoot nation. My name is Jamie Bains. I am the head of this outfit. We ask permission to cross your land to take these cattle north of the medicine line to Canada." The trail boss did his best to appear calm.

One of the young men translated so all of the warriors could understand. They talked among themselves, and then the translator turned and addressed them. "Blackfoot land is not for crossing."

Again Jamie spoke, trying to express things clearly so there would be no misunderstanding. "We are taking the herd north into the foothills country of Canada, to Fort Macleod. The cattle are for the redcoats, members of the North West

Mounted Police. The redcoats are your friends. We ask for safe passage across your land."

The young trail boss waited while his words were translated. Younger warriors were already getting restless and impatient. Again a tingle of fear went down his spine.

Finally the reply was given by the translator. "There are few buffalo. A great hunger has come among the Blackfoot. We need cattle."

Jamie glanced at the others. At least they were putting forward their demands. He replied cautiously. "These cattle were owned by Patrick McNeil. He was a redcoat who was a friend of Chief Crowfoot and many of the Blackfoot. Patrick was killed by outlaws, and we are taking the herd to Canada for him."

Again there was a translation. The older chief seemed particularly concerned. This time the reply was friendlier. "The Blackfoot know the redcoat you call Patrick McNeil. They want to punish those who killed him."

Jamie glanced around and saw that Billy had joined them. "The man who killed him has already been punished. We ask to be allowed to take Patrick's cattle across Blackfoot land to the redcoats in Canada."

After the translation the reply finally came. "We honour the name of the redcoat Patrick McNeil, but the Blackfoot are hungry. We ask that you give us twenty-five cattle for the right to cross Blackfoot land."

The trail boss looked at the others for a moment. Twenty-five head of cattle would bankrupt the whole enterprise, but they were at least bargaining. They had to be reasonable. "The redcoats will not let the Blackfoot starve. Once the herd is delivered to them in Fort Macleod they will help to feed you. All I can offer is two steers for the right to cross Blackfoot land."

The translator did not even bother to put Jamie's offer to the others before he said. "Two steers are not enough. We want more."

Jamie paused as he tried to think. Time was on their side. "I have to talk to the others before I can offer more," he said clearly. "I will return."

The boy turned his horse and rode back towards the place where Lee had stopped the chuck wagon. The others followed him, leaving the Blackfoot to wait. Already a fire was burning, and the cook was preparing coffee. Jamie dismounted and went to sit on a wooden case that had been set on the ground.

"What are you gonna do, Mister Jamie?" Josh asked.

The trail boss waited for a moment before answering. He was now convinced that if they did not lose their nerve time would work to their advantage. "We are going to wait," he finally told the others. "Let the cattle graze but keep a close check on them. Don't let the Blackfoot get their hands on any of them."

Chisholm was clearly worried. "But shouldn't we be doing somethin'?"

"What?"

"I don't know, but we can't just sit here."

"We wait," said Jamie firmly. "We are just going to sit here and wait. They are going to grow tired."

"But why did you say you wanted the chance to talk to us?" The Texan was nervously fiddling with the gun in his holster.

Jamie looked at the others circling him, waiting on his every word. There was the hint of panic in his crew, and he had to try and calm them. "I know enough about the Blackfoot people to understand that they believe that everyone should talk and agree before action is taken. When I said I had to talk to the rest of you they understood that, but I've already made up my mind about what to do."

"What's that?" Chisholm demanded.

"We wait and wear them down until they become more reasonable."

"That ain't no plan!"

Buck was close to being frantic. "It just gives 'em time to organize an attack on us."

"I don't think they're going to attack," said the trail boss.

"How can you be sure?"

"I can't."

Billy had been listening intently. "But what's the plan?"

"We wait. Let's drink some coffee. Time is on our side."

The cowboys were confused and frustrated. What sort of a trail boss did they have? The Blackfoot warriors had spread out around them so that they now circled the herd. The cowboys and the herd felt trapped, vulnerable. At any moment young warriors could attack, and drive off part of the herd, and they could do nothing.

Chisholm paced back and forth looking at the Blackfoot and then back at the young trail boss. "We've got to do somethin'."

"Like what?" Jamie asked.

"We could be wiped out!"

"They won't attack."

"How do you know?"

"Because they gave us time to talk. They're honourable."

Buck had been listening intently. "They ain't honourable. They're plannin' out their attack right now, I bet."

"What do you suggest, Buck?"

"We should get 'em first before they get us!"

"You must want to die," the trail boss said sternly. "The first shot you get off we'll have so many arrows sticking out

of us we'd look like porcupines. We wait. In time they will
grow tired."

The talk came to an end. Their leader had given his
orders. There was nothing more to be said, but Jamie knew all
of the cowboys felt uneasy. They murmured to each other,
complaining that all this was just giving the Blackfoot time to
collect more warriors, but through it all the young trail boss
sat calmly watching the scene, waiting.

Billy was the only one who held his tongue. He studied
the Blackfoot riding around them like they were on guard,
and then he looked at the trail boss sitting unruffled, like
nothing out of the ordinary was happening.

"What do you think?" whispered Kate to Billy so the
others would not hear.

"That brother of yours sure is a calm cool one."

"Jamie always tries to think things through."

Billy was looking out at the Blackfoot. "Those Indians
look fierce, but maybe they're just tryin' to frighten us. Does
Jamie know somethin' more about the Blackfoot that he's not
tellin' us about?"

"I don't know."

"I just hope he knows what he's doin'."

"Why do you care, Billy?" Kate asked suddenly. "You
should be happy to see us attacked."

"They'll kill me along with everybody else, Kate."

The girl walked away. Kate knew that if she stayed
around the fire she would be drawn into an argument by one
of the cowboys, and what could she say to defend Jamie? She
did not understand his plan any more than any of the others.
All she knew was that she had to have faith in her brother.

For two hours Jamie sat around the fire calmly eating a
big meal and then drinking coffee, the staple drink of all
cowboys. No one spoke much. The usual jokes and banter
were gone. They still kept to a routine. Cowboys rotated those

on watch so that everyone would have the chance to eat around the campfire, but everyone was quiet and uneasy. The undercurrent of fear made them all nervous.

Around them the Blackfoot guarded the cowboys impatiently. The warriors stayed on their ponies fingering their weapons as if expecting trouble to break out at any moment. Some looked like they would welcome a fight but nothing happened.

Finally Jamie got to his feet and said to the others. "Let's go and see if they will accept our new offer."

Again they mounted up and Jamie, Chisholm, Josh and Kate rode out to meet the Blackfoot. Only about seventy warriors rode to meet them, but the chief with the long hair and sharp nose was among them. The trail boss made a quick estimate and decided that at least thirty of the Blackfoot had grown tired of the stalemate and had already ridden off. He wondered if his plan was working.

The two sides again met each other on horseback. Jamie held up his hand in greeting. The chief was out in front, and the translator waited impatiently.

The young trail boss started slowly. "We have talked long and hard about this. Some of the cowboys think we should give nothing. But I have argued that the Blackfoot are a fair and honourable people. We are crossing their land, and we should pay the Blackfoot nation something, but twenty-five head of cattle is too much. After much talk I have got my people to agree to pay three head of cattle to cross Blackfoot land. Three steers, no more."

Jamie paused and waited while his words were translated. He could see the mounting annoyance of the chiefs and young braves. When the translation was complete he began talking again.

"When we get the herd of cattle north into Canada, and deliver them, the redcoats will give some steers to your people, but I cannot afford to give any more than three head of cattle for the right to cross Blackfoot land."

Again Jamie stopped and again the translation took place. This time the Blackfoot began to argue among themselves. The boy had no idea what it all meant. Finally the discussion came to an end and the translator addressed them again.

"The Blackfoot are not pleased. To cross Blackfoot land they demand at least fifteen head of cattle."

Jamie smiled to himself. They were beginning to reduce their demands. He glanced at Chisholm and Josh before replying. "No. That is too much. Remember that Patrick McNeil, the redcoat, was the friend of the Blackfoot. He helped your people many times. We are willing to pay, but I am asking that you be reasonable in your demands."

Again there was more talk among the Blackfoot before the translator turned back to them. "Ten head of cattle. That's what we ask. The people of the Blackfoot nation are hungry."

Jamie was prompt in his reply. "No. That is too much, but I think the men will agree to four head of cattle. No more."

After some discussion the word came back through the translator. "We want ten cattle."

Jamie turned to Chisholm and Josh. "What do you think?" he asked quietly so the translator would not hear.

"Ten head. Maybe that's reasonable," Chisholm replied.

"What do you think, Josh?"

"I sure wouldn't want my curly locks on one of 'em poles they carry."

"And you, Kate?"

"They're hungry, Jamie. Maybe we should give them the ten head."

The young trail boss looked across to the Blackfoot. "Ten head of cattle is too much," he announced in a loud voice. "I have to go back to talk to the others. We all have to agree."

There was more talk, but the two sides could not come to an agreement. Jamie turned his horse and rode back towards the others around the fire. When they dismounted Kate was not happy.

"Why do you have to talk to the others?" she demanded. "The three of us all agreed that we should give them ten head."

"Ten head is too many."

"You didn't even listen to what we said to you."

Jamie nodded solemnly. "You're right, Kate."

The whole crew was listening to the brother and sister argue. "What's wrong with you? We could get in deep trouble."

"We have to play it out a little longer, and the longer we wait the less they will demand."

Finally she understood Jamie's plan. "You mean, like, you're just waiting to wear them down hoping that they will reduce their demands?"

"They are already growing tired. We have to wait until we strike a deal that both the Blackfoot and ourselves will see as a victory. We're not quite there yet."

"But isn't that unfair?"

"I don't think so. Would it have been fair for us to give them the twenty-five head at the beginning? What if they had accepted our offer of two head? What's fair?"

"I don't know, but ..." She was not sure what to believe at this point.

"If we wait just a little longer maybe we can get an agreement that both sides think is fair."

Jamie looked at the others. All of them were now unsure what to believe. Of the whole group only Billy had a soft smile on his face. Maybe he was the only one who understood clearly what was happening.

The cowboys went back to drinking coffee as they sat around the fire. They still nervously watched the Blackfoot, who circled them in their restless way. For more than an hour they waited. The sun was dipping down towards the mountains in the west when the trail boss again got to his feet.

"Let's go and talk," he announced simply.

Again Jamie led the delegation along with Chisholm, Josh and Kate. The Blackfoot hurried to assemble their group. This time there were less than forty warriors who rode up to meet with them, but the older chief was still with them. Jamie reined in and held up his hand as a sign of peace. Again he spoke in a loud voice to the mounted members of the Blackfoot nation.

"We have spoken at great lengths about your offer for crossing Blackfoot land. There is much disagreement among my people. I have had to argue that the Blackfoot should be paid something to cross their land but not all agree. Finally I said to them that we should offer five head of cattle. Five. We think that is fair."

The discussion among the Blackfoot went on a long time before the translator finally came back to him. "For a young boy you drive a hard bargain with the Blackfoot," the translator began. "Our people are hungry. We ask for more."

Jamie knew that the bargaining was over. In his speech he tried to be generous. "The Blackfoot are a great nation of many proud warriors and many teepees. The buffalo have vanished and that has left the people hungry. But still you ask for what you think is fair. Rather than five steers I will give you six of my best animals for the right to cross Blackfoot land. Six steers. Please remember us and the redcoat, Patrick McNeil, as friends who tried to help you in your time of need."

When the translation was completed, the chief gave a sign of agreement. Jamie gave the order. Josh and Chisholm rode towards the herd. In a moment six steers had been cut out and were delivered to the Blackfoot. The last they saw of the cattle, they were being chased by young warriors up into the hills. There would be feasting in the teepees that night.

15

The Blackfoot disappeared as quickly as they had come, and the cowboys and their herd were left alone in the vast foothills country. Already the sun was beginning to make streaks of gold and red in the western sky. The day was almost over.

Jamie felt as if a huge burden had been lifted from his shoulders. He went among the men gathered around the fire and briefly explained what had happened.

It was Trapper who expressed the thoughts of most of the crew. "You done well, Mister Jamie," he said simply.

"That's a fact," agreed Josh. "You have nerves of steel."

Jamie smiled. Praise from these rough cowboys was something to be remembered.

They talked for a time, letting the tension of the day ease away, and then the young trail boss issued simple orders. "We'll stay here for the night and resume the drive at sunup. It's only a few days before we cross the border into the Canadian foothills country."

Mike and Trapper took the first watch and rode around the herd singing songs to the cattle while the rest of the crew sat around the campfire talking. But not all of the cowboys were pleased with the results. Buck was particularly vocal about his dissatisfaction.

"Why'd we have to give them any cattle at all?" he told others around the fire. "This is a free country. We should be able to go anywhere we want."

Kate was annoyed that he refused to understand. "Because it's their land, Buck."

"Indians don't own land like us white folk."

Kate's impatience showed. "This area is their country. They deserve to be paid if we want to cross it. The truth is that you're frightened of the Blackfoot."

"I am not!"

"You and Fergie came running back like dogs with your tails between your legs." She knew she was calling him a coward, but she did not care.

"I ain't afraid of no Indian. Not never!"

It was Billy who headed off the argument. "I think the trail boss did well. Mister Jamie had a plan, and he stuck with it, and it paid off. If he refused to give the Blackfoot any cattle they would have attacked and taken what they wanted. And if he had agreed to give twenty-five head in the beginning they would have been back for more. Making them wait made them reduce their demands."

Jamie said nothing, but he could see that Billy had understood his strategy and understood that the plan had worked. Still the trail boss said nothing to him. In his mind, Billy was an outlaw who had to be punished.

After supper, when the cowboys were settling for the night, Billy came over to talk to Kate. She was the only one of the outfit who would talk to him. In the last few days they had come to share a lot.

"Have you finished your work?" she asked.

"When this drive is over I'll be happy to see the end of pots and pans."

"But what's going to happen to you then, Billy?"

He shrugged but said nothing.

They sat leaning up against their bedrolls and looking into the fire. Each of them had a night pony saddled and tethered close by. Jamie and a few other cowboys were already in their bedrolls sleeping while others chatted quietly.

All of them except Kate and Lee would take their turn on watch that night.

"Jamie tells me that we'll be at Fort Macleod in a few days," Kate said quietly. "You know what that means for you when we get there."

"I'm not lookin' forward to it." The boy closed his eyes as if trying to keep the image from his mind.

"It's not going to be good for you. Cattle rustling, Patrick's murder, when the court hears that ..." Kate's words petered out.

"Do you think the judge will go hard on me, Kate?"

"They don't like outlaws in Canada, especially ones from south of the border." She paused for a moment and then added. "They could hang you for your crimes, Billy."

"Yes, I know," he said quietly.

The two of them stared into the fire for the longest time. The glow of the flames lit a small area and beyond was the darkness of night. The flickering light reflected on their faces.

Kate propped herself up on one elbow. "You don't really have to go to court, Billy."

"What do you mean?"

"In the middle of the night you could get on your horse and just ride south and never come back," she whispered.

"Do you think so?"

"You could take some food: salt pork, beans and biscuits, coffee. Lee would never notice that it was gone. You could ride back the way that we came, following our trail. In a few days you'd be among strangers. They'd never know any of this happened."

"Jamie would come after me or send someone to hunt me down."

"I don't think so. Anyway you could keep riding south: Texas, California, even Mexico. They'd never find you there."

"Just run, you mean. Keep on running."

"If you go to Canada you're gonna be sent to jail for a long time, Billy. Or there's a good chance that you'll be hung for your part in Patrick's murder. If you leave now you can be free, away from all of this. You can make a new life for yourself."

Billy put his hands behind his head and stretched out on the ground. "Free. I'd like that. I've been runnin' most of my life. The funny thing is the more I run the less free I become. It feels like everyone is after me and behind every tree someone is waitin' to capture me."

"It's your only chance, Billy. Wait until the middle of the night. When you mount up the others will think that you're going to take a watch, but you just keep on riding south. By dawn you'll be miles away, and by nightfall tomorrow you'll be fifty miles south. No one will go after you."

"Do you really think I should do it?"

"Better that than going to jail or being hanged."

Billy lay motionless looking into the fire for a long time before he answered. "You know Kate, I've been runnin' for a long time. Runnin' from home, runnin' from people I worked for, runnin' from sheriffs and mounted police, runnin' from ranchers and cattle drovers. I'm tired of runnin'. If I leave now and ride south I'll always be an outlaw, always runnin'." He paused, staring into the fire.

"Then what do you want to do?"

"I guess seeing McCoy killed and meeting you and Jamie and the others made me understand that I don't want to live like this any more. I want to change. I'd like to be someone like Jamie. That's funny. When I first met Jamie I hated him. He seemed to have everything, and I had nothing."

"We had no more than you, Billy."

"I know that now. I really messed things up. But now I admire Jamie more than anyone for being able to bring this herd of cattle north into the foothills country. I admire him, but he still hates me."

Again Billy was quiet. The fire crackled as it burned. Kate waited a long time for him to gather his thoughts. Finally he began again.

"I guess, Kate, I'm gonna go up to Canada, and I'm gonna face the judge, and I'm gonna take what he gives to me 'cause I don't want to be runnin' anymore."

Kate watched the dancing flames of the fire for a long time before finally answering. "If that's what you want, Billy, then so be it then."

The two got out their bedrolls and got ready for the night. Billy slept over by the chuck wagon and Kate spread her bedroll beside her brother. The other cowboys slept peacefully in the warm summer evening.

The fire burned low, and Kate could see the billions of stars sparkling like jewels in the firmament. The cattle grazed contentedly, and in the distance she could hear the cowboys singing mournful songs to the cattle.

What was going to happen to Billy? Part of her wished he would just ride south and disappear into the vast empty wilderness that lay on every side of them. But he was making a choice, and she would have to respect it. He was choosing to change his life, even though there was a good chance that the penalty for his crimes might ruin him. As she was thinking about this Kate drifted off to sleep.

The crack of a rifle shot shattered the stillness of the early morning light. Then came another shot and another. The shots were followed by the thundering of hooves and then shouts and curses.

Jamie was up and into the saddle of his stallion in one bound. The whole crew was right behind him. He raced to the opposite side of the herd in the direction the shots had come from. There he found Buck and Fergie shouting after three disappearing steers. Behind the steers a half a dozen young Blackfoot were yelling as they drove the cattle up into the hills.

"Blackfoot raiders! We're goin' after 'em!" Buck was shouting.

"Who shot their weapon?" Jamie demanded.

Fergie's horse was dancing about excitedly. "Buck and I fired at 'em, but they got clean away."

"My orders were that there was to be no firing!" Jamie was furious.

"They're cattle raiders," Buck shouted.

"If you kill one of the Blackfoot, hundreds of them will come looking for revenge."

"They ain't gonna get us. They're just Indians. We're goin' after them cattle."

"Stay put, Buck!" the trail boss ordered. The rest of the crew had quickly gathered. The eastern sky was already getting light. The sun would be over the horizon in a few minutes.

"You aimin' to let them cattle go to them Indians?"

"Buck, it's dangerous to ride up there. You won't have a chance."

"Well that'll show that sister of yours that we ain't afraid of no Indians. Not Fergie and Bucko. No way."

"Are you determined to kill yourself?" Jamie was losing patience.

"I could have told you that you couldn't trust the thievin' redskins. Come on, Fergie. Let's go and teach 'em a lesson!"

Jamie looked at the others gathered around on their horses. Josh was there with Chisholm, waiting to see how he would handle these two difficult cowboys. Billy looked the most concerned of all. Beside the outlaw was his sister Kate and the rest of the crew.

"You aren't going anywhere, Buck."

"You're scared, boy? Scared of a bunch o' Indians?"

"I'm not stupid."

"You're a coward, boy. Come on, Fergie. Let's go after them Indians before they get away."

Jamie pulled his long rifle out of its holster. He cocked it and then held it on his thigh with the barrel pointing at the sky. "You're not goin' anywhere, Buck. I'm not gonna risk this whole cattle drive because you were insulted by my sister and want to prove yourself a man."

Buck looked at him scornfully. "You wouldn't know how to use that gun. You're a weak one, just a boy. We're goin' after them cattle, ain't we, Fergie?"

"Damned right."

"Maybe he can't use his gun but I can." It was Billy. He had a rifle in his hand, and he was pointing it right at Buck.

"This ain't your fight, boy."

"It is now. Mister Jamie's right. If you go and kill some Blackfoot then the whole tribe will come down on us, and we'll never get through to Canada."

"You ain't gonna use that gun."

Billy smiled nervously. "Then try me out, Buck, but remember I'm already a condemned man. I'm going to go before a judge in Canada charged with helpin' to kill a man. What have I got to lose? One more killin' against me is not gonna make a difference."

Buck looked nervously from Fergie to Jamie and back to Billy again. The outlaw boy never wavered, never lowered his rifle, never showed a moment of doubt. The cold determination showed Billy meant business.

"All right boy, all right. Lower that rifle. Don't shoot. I'm not goin' nowheres."

Even Jamie was relieved to see Billy lower the rifle. "Let's go back to the camp. Lee will have something cooking on the fire."

As they started to ride back towards the chuck wagon, Buck continued to talk. "But didn't I tell you that them Indians would steal you blind, Mister Jamie. They are up to no good." But no one paid any attention to him. Jamie was more concerned about how Billy got the rifle, but somehow even that did not matter much any more.

It was an hour later, when they were getting ready to move the cattle out, that Buck's prediction about the Indians was proven wrong.

"Look, Mister Jamie," Chisholm called.

The three head of cattle that had been stolen were being driven back to the herd by a group of about ten Blackfoot warriors. The trail boss could barely believe his eyes. The three steers came up at a trot and merged into the herd as if they were glad to be a part of it again.

Jamie rode over to talk to the Blackfoot. He recognized the translator and the chief from the negotiations the day before. The trail boss reined in, and they talked.

"Chief Crowfoot regrets the actions of the young warriors," the translator began. "He cannot control the high spirits of all our young people. He returns the cattle because an agreement had been made, and Crowfoot always keeps his word."

"Thank you for returning them. We need all the cattle." Then Jamie asked, "Is this Crowfoot, the great Blackfoot chief?"

"Yes," he replied. "Crowfoot, friend of the redcoats and Patrick McNeil."

16

The remainder of the cattle drive into Canada was uneventful. Often they saw Blackfoot warriors out on the hunt, or families travelling with all of their belongings tied to travois, pulled by ponies. But always the cowboys on the drive were treated with courtesy and respect.

One fine summer morning Jamie was riding out in front of the herd when he came across a surveyor's cairn marking the international border between Canada and the United States. He rode back to tell Kate, and the two of them went on to inspect the simple mound of rocks. Both felt a sense of pride and relief to be back home again.

The Canadian foothills were luxuriant with grass. To the west they could see the jagged, snow-covered peaks of the Rocky Mountains that stretched in a long unbroken chain from north to south. The foothills rolled in an uneven way up to the very base of the mountains. There, abruptly, the grasslands stopped and forests of aspen and fir began.

The cattle moved through the country, browsing on the grass as the drive continued. Jamie was enough of a cattleman to know that this was some of the richest grazing land that they had seen. He knew that the cattle they had brought north would thrive and prosper in this country.

But as the herd moved slowly north the young trail boss thought more and more about Billy. He was struck by how calm the outlaw had become after he had confronted Buck. Jamie tried to talk to Kate about him, but her only response was to suggest that he talk directly to Billy. That was a hard thing for Jamie. There was still bad blood between them.

The evening after they crossed the border he saw Billy washing pots and pans near the chuck wagon. Kate was helping him. The trail boss walked over to the two of them and stood awkwardly for a moment before he began. "Billy, I've been thinking. We're not far from Fort Macleod now."

Billy took his hands out of the soapy water. "Yes?"

"Maybe the two of us should ride ahead and see the mounted police."

"When do you want to go?" Billy asked simply.

"Tomorrow at sunup."

"I'll be ready."

"Are you willing to come with me and face the judge?" Jamie asked.

Billy nodded. "I have to do it."

Jamie looked at the boy, trying to understand what he meant. "We'll head out tomorrow morning," he said simply and then turned to go.

"And Jamie," Kate added decisively. "I'm going with you."

"Why?"

She frowned in her determined way. "I'm coming. That's all. And no one's gonna stop me."

Jamie nodded. He knew there was no arguing with his sister when she made up her mind.

That evening the trail boss talked to Josh and Chisholm, putting them in charge of the drive. The next morning after breakfast, while the cowboys were taking their positions around the herd, Kate, Billy and Jamie set out. Their route took them across the Milk River, and then they picked up a trail leading north. Jamie knew from his map that it would take them to Fort Macleod.

As the day wore on their horses stretched out into an easy loping run that ate up the miles. There were no mosquitoes and fewer bull flies, but the grasshoppers flew before their horses like a coming plague. Towards midday the summer sun turned hot. They stopped for lunch and a short rest beside a creek, but before long they were into the saddle again, riding north.

No one spoke much. Kate worried about Billy while Jamie wondered what should be the proper thing to happen once they got to Fort Macleod. The calmest of the three of them was Billy. His fate was soon to be determined, and yet he seemed to face it without a hint of fear.

The shadows were lengthening, and their horses were about played out, when they spotted the buildings of Fort Macleod. It was not long before they were riding down the dusty street of the frontier town. Then they crossed the wooden bridge to a small island in the middle of the Oldman River, where the fort had been built.

Jamie led the others through the gates of the palisaded fort and into the parade ground. They were still on their horses when a scarlet-coated constable of the North West Mounted Police confronted them. "Please state your business," the officer demanded in a formal manner.

Jamie spoke for the others. "I have brought in a prisoner accused of cattle rustling and involved in a murder," he said calmly.

"Murder! That's a serious charge. Who was murdered?"

"Patrick McNeil. The former North West Mounted Police constable."

"Patrick killed?" The policeman was shocked. "Why, he was one of my best friends!"

They had climbed off their horses. "And ours too. He was a good man."

"Who killed him?"

"An outlaw called McCoy," Jamie explained. "His partner was Billy, here."

The scarlet-coated policeman recoiled in shock. "A murderer! But he's not even tied up!"

"I didn't think it was necessary."

The policeman was suddenly angry. "If this boy's had a part in killing Patrick McNeil he's going to hang!" In a moment his handcuffs were on Billy's wrists, and he grasped him hard at the elbow so the boy could not make a break for freedom.

"You don't need to handcuff him, sir," said Kate, meekly.

The policeman turned on her. There was raw anger in his eyes. "It's the gallows for him if the magistrate finds this boy guilty. Killing a policeman is a serious matter in this country!"

The constable wrenched Billy almost off his feet and pulled him roughly towards the jailhouse. Over his shoulder he delivered orders to the others. "Once I get this murderer into a cell the two of you will swear out an information saying what happened. Tomorrow morning he will appear in front of Magistrate Macleod. If he's found guilty he'll be swinging if I know the judge."

Inside Billy was pushed into a prison cell. The metal door squeaked as it closed and then clanged shut ominously. In a small office the policeman wrote out Jamie's explanation of the events leading up to the murder and had him sign the statement at the bottom of the page.

"What's going to happen now?" Kate asked.

The constable looked at her sternly. "Billy will appear at ten o'clock tomorrow morning in front of Magistrate Macleod. You are both required to be there."

There was nothing else they could do. A gloominess had descended on Jamie and Kate as they mounted their horses. Kate trailed Billy's pony, and they rode out of the fort. Jamie led them up the Oldman River a distance until they found a grove of trees. There they made camp, turned their horses loose, made something to eat and settled in for the night.

They were sitting around the campfire when Kate asked. "Do you really think that they are going to hang Billy?"

"I don't know."

"It wouldn't be fair to hang him. It was McCoy's fault. He got Billy into trouble."

"It's wrong to blame someone else, Kate. Billy is responsible for his actions."

"But he's changed, Jamie and I believe him when he says that he had nothing to do with Patrick's death."

They sat, looking into the fire for a long time. Both felt a sense of desolation. Finally Kate asked her brother. "What are you going to say tomorrow?"

"I'm going to tell the truth. It's up to the magistrate to decide."

"I feel sorry for Billy."

"I know you do, Kate. I know."

They finished their meal in silence and let the fire burn down to embers. For the first time in weeks they did not have to think about cattle or the drive. Now their worries were different but even more troublesome.

The warm summer evening gathered about them as shadows spread across the land. In the west the sun glinted off the snow on the mountain peaks and then slowly sunk behind them. A quiet hush descended upon them. A gentle breeze stirred the trees and long grass, and one by one the stars came out in the darkening sky. The two of them settled into their bedrolls for a fitful, anxious sleep.

The next morning they were waiting at the primitive log hut that served as a courthouse when the doors were opened at ten. Inside there were benches for spectators, a raised platform for the judge's desk, a Union Jack standing in a corner and beside it a portrait of Queen Victoria. News of the trial must have spread rapidly through the frontier town because the courtroom was packed.

A red-coated police constable came into the room and called out in a loud voice. "All rise! All rise!" The spectators leaped to their feet. A moment later a distinguished-looking man wearing a long black robe swept into the room. "Magistrate Colonel James Macleod presiding." When the magistrate took his seat Kate and Jamie, along with the other spectators, settled onto the benches.

The magistrate shuffled some papers that were in front of him. Some routine matters of the court were dealt with, and then Billy's case was called. There was a buzz of expectation. The prisoner, with his hands shackled together, was led into the room by the North West Mounted Police constable who had arrested him. As he was led to the dock, Billy searched the courtroom until he saw Kate and Jamie sitting in the front row of spectators. Seeing the two of them seemed to give him a sense of relief.

The charges were read out by a black-suited clerk. "... and you did steal cattle, the property of Patrick McNeil, and you were an accomplice to the murder of Patrick McNeil. How do you answer to these charges: guilty or not guilty?"

Billy squared his shoulders. "I don't know, sir. I didn't have anything to do with the murder of Mister Patrick."

"Are you sure?" asked the magistrate.

"I wasn't even there when he was killed."

"All right, I'll enter your plea as not guilty. Let's hear the evidence."

The clerk looked at the papers in front of him and then announced: "Mister Jamie Bains has given this information. Is Mister Bains in the court?"

Jamie got to his feet. "Yes, sir. I am Jamie Bains." He was ushered to the witness box where he swore to tell the truth with his hand on the Bible.

The judge leaned forward and looked intently at the witness. "Tell me, Mister Bains. Is this matter about the murder of the former North West Mounted Police Constable Patrick McNeil?"

"Yes, sir."

"I am sorry to hear that. I knew him well. Constable McNeil was one of the best men in the force."

Jamie had a sinking feeling. This would not be good for Billy.

Magistrate Macleod continued. "Tell me the circumstances of his death."

Jamie started slowly. He explained how Patrick had arrested McCoy and Billy and then described how he and his sister had joined Patrick to go to Kohrs' Ranch and bring the herd north into Canada.

When he came to the part of the cattle rustling and murder the magistrate asked a number of detailed questions. He wanted to know exactly where everyone was at the time of the killing. Jamie explained he did not witness the killing. He wanted to tell the truth and let the judge make up his mind about Billy.

At the end of the round of questioning the magistrate asked Jamie a pointed question. "Are you satisfied in your own mind, Mister Bains, that it was McCoy, rather than this defendant, who killed Patrick McNeil?"

"Yes, sir."

The magistrate paused for a moment before saying: "I have to conclude that there is no evidence that the accused was involved in the planning of the killing or in the killing itself." He paused again before adding, "All right. Go on, Mister Bains."

Jamie described how they continued the drive through the land of the Blackfoot confederacy, and he explained that the herd would be arriving at Fort Macleod in a couple of days.

The magistrate leaned back in his chair and looked at the boy in the witness box. "You are to be commended, Mister Bains. The Blackfoot and the people of this community need that herd of cattle to survive the coming winter. We also compliment you on bringing this outlaw to trial. He obviously is a desperate person living the life of crime who must be dealt with by the full measure of the law. Thank you for your testimony. You may be excused."

As Jamie left the witness box he had a horrible sinking feeling. He had set out to tell the truth, but all the evidence pointed to the conclusion that Billy was an outlaw who must be punished harshly.

Magistrate Macleod shuffled his papers again before he addressed the court. When he began there was a dark, ominous quality to his voice that suggested that he had already decided to make an example of Billy.

"There is a lawlessness on this frontier that must be stopped, and I intend to stop it. When a fine, law-abiding young man like Patrick McNeil is murdered in cold blood it is more than a personal tragedy; it is an act that does damage to our whole community. We need men like him — brave men willing to take risks. When men such as this are cut down in the prime of life by outlaws, we must rise up as a community and punish them with the full measure of the law."

Kate felt a panic in the very core of her being. Billy was to be condemned — hung on the gallows until he was dead. She was sure of it now. Despite her feelings for Patrick, she knew that she had to do everything in her power to stop it.

"Mister Magistrate, your honour, sir," Kate blurted out. She was on her feet now. "Please sir, let me speak," she pleaded. There was a loud murmur from the spectators.

The magistrate looked up at the room. His face showed annoyance. "Who are you to disturb my court?"

Panic made her tremble all over. "I am Kate Bains, sir, Jamie's sister."

"Do you have anything to add to his testimony?"

"Yes sir, I have."

He studied her critically for a moment. "All right, swear her in, but I hope you have something worthwhile to tell the court."

Kate tried to stay calm as she walked to the witness box. The black-robed magistrate sat grim faced; Billy stood at the dock, his wrists shackled; the crowd of spectators leaned forward in expectation.

"Do you swear to tell the truth, the whole truth and nothing but the truth?" the clerk demanded.

Kate screwed up her courage. "I do."

"Tell me what you know about this matter, Miss Bains," asked the magistrate.

"Billy has changed, Your Honour. He's no longer an outlaw. You can't hang him, sir. It just wouldn't be right."

"He's done terrible things, Miss Bains. He admits it himself. Would you deny the facts?"

"No, sir." Kate felt tears well up in her eyes. "But ... but he's really sorry for what he has done and wants to make amends."

"How can he bring back Patrick McNeil?"

"He can't. Nothing can change that." Kate wiped her face with the back of her hand, smearing tears across her cheeks. "But he came here to Canada to face up to his crime. He could have run away. When we were on the drive he could have got on his horse and rode away and none of us could have caught him. But he didn't. He came here to stand before you and admit that he had done wrong and take his punishment. You've got to believe me, Your Honour, sir. Billy has changed."

The more Kate talked the more confident she became. "He chose to come to Fort Macleod. And ... and there is one other thing. Some of the cowboys in the drive were angry that Blackfoot had stolen cattle. It was Billy who stopped them from raiding the Blackfoot camps."

The magistrate leaned across his desk. "They wanted to attack the Blackfoot? That could have started an Indian War. Is that true, Mister Bains?"

Jamie got to his feet. "Yes, sir. It is true. Billy risked his own life to stop the raid on the Blackfoot."

"And what do you think about Billy, Mister Bains?" the magistrate demanded.

Jamie looked at his sister in the witness box and then at the prisoner standing in the dock. Billy's steady gaze suggested that the trail boss' opinion of him was more important than anything else to him. There was not a sound from the spectators. Everything depended on what Jamie was about to say.

"Kate's right, sir. Billy is different than the person we first met. Patrick McNeil's killing was a great loss to us, but taking Billy's life won't bring him back. Billy has faced up to the things that he has done wrong. He helped us get the cattle north into Canada. I came to rely on him."

The magistrate studied his papers for a long time before looking up again. "And you, Miss Bains? What do you think?"

"You've got to give him another chance, Mister Magistrate, sir. Billy will grow up to be a good man. I know it. I think even Patrick, if he were alive today, would have wanted him to have another chance."

"Thank you, Miss Bains. You can leave the witness box."

Kate rejoined her brother and the two sat on the edge of the hard wooden bench, straining to hear.

The magistrate studied his papers for the longest time. There was a hush in the courtroom. The prisoner stood alone at the dock, waiting for his future to be decided. Then the magistrate looked at Billy and addressed him for the first time.

"Do you have anything to say?"

Billy looked at his friends and then at the magistrate without wavering. "What I did was wrong, sir, and I deserve whatever punishment I am given. More than anything else I wish I could bring back Patrick McNeil, but that's not possible. All I can do is live the rest of my life trying to make up for the mistakes I have made."

Quiet descended on the courtroom. The magistrate looked at his papers again and then addressed the assembled crowd with a slow but firm voice.

"These are serious charges, charges most men would be hung for. But there are many things to think about here. The prisoner helped to bring the cattle north and helped to stop a raid on the Blackfoot, which could well have caused a war, given the delicate nature of things at the moment. He came to this court and voluntarily admitted that he had done wrong. But I think the most important thing is that he has two friends who say that he has changed and has become a person of good character."

The magistrate paused for a long time. The packed courtroom waited in anticipation. Billy stood in the prisoner's dock without flinching. Then the magistrate looked up. "Would Mister Jamie Bains and Miss Kate Bains please stand up."

Jamie and Kate cautiously got to their feet. "Yes, sir," they both said at the same time.

"Are you planning to stay in the foothills country, Mister Bains?"

Jamie was taken back. "Yes I … I have been thinking I would take the remainder of the herd and try to be a rancher here in the foothills country."

"I see ..." Again the magistrate studied his papers. The spectators waited expectantly. When he looked up there was a resolute look to his face. He began his speech slowly.

"There is no evidence that the prisoner took part in the murder of the unfortunate Patrick McNeil. He is guilty of cattle rustling, but all of the cattle were recovered. We would be a poor country if we could not temper our judgments with mercy — especially mercy for one who admits his mistakes and asks forgiveness."

The magistrate suddenly turned to Jamie. "I'd like to turn the prisoner into your care, Mister Bains, if you will have him. Maybe the two of you can help to make this land prosper. What's your answer?"

Jamie looked at his sister and then across the room to Billy in the prisoner's box. "Yes, sir. Yes. I'd like to work with Billy. I think we can build a good life here in the foothills country."

"We need people like you in this community. We need cattle. This country needs to be developed. The prisoner will be released into the custody of Jamie Bains; he will report each month to the chief constable of Fort Macleod; and he will live an exemplary life. If he fails he will be dealt with by the full power of the law."

There was a gasp from the spectators. "So ordered!" and the magistrate's gavel hammered his desk, indicating that the case was at an end.

17

Billy's release was so unexpected that they could hardly comprehend it. Papers were signed, the shackles were taken off Billy's wrists, and he walked out of the courtroom a free man.

In the yard of the fort Billy tried to find some way to express his appreciation. "I ... I don't know how you managed do it."

"We just told the truth, Billy," Kate replied.

"You saved yourself," Jamie added. "Your actions showed that deep down you're a good person."

"No. You saved me. Both of you saved me."

Jamie felt embarrassed. "Come on. Let's go and find that herd of ours."

The trail boss laughed as he swung up onto the back of his stallion. Then the others joined him. All of them felt an enormous sense of relief at the sentence given by the magistrate.

As they rode out of town, past the merchants' stores, frame houses and sod huts they saw people pointing and talking about them. News travelled fast in a small town. Already they had made their mark on this country.

By nightfall they had found the others, and after another day of the drive they settled the herd on lush pasture west of town on the south bank of the Oldman River. The next day Jamie made arrangements for Mr. Sweeney, the buyer for the I.G. Baker Company of Fort Macleod, a branch of the Fort Benton merchants that they had visited three months before, to come out and look at the herd.

Sweeney was most complimentary. "Those are the best-lookin' animals I've seen in these parts. There's a real shortage of cattle, boy. I'll buy every head."

"Only the steers are for sale," Jamie told him.

"Then I'll take all the steers, boy."

Jamie bristled. "The name's Bains, not boy. Mister Jamie Bains."

Sweeney was most apologetic. "Yes, sir, Mister Bains. And it's a pleasure to do business with you, sir."

The sale of the steers was enough to pay off the loan Patrick had taken from Conrad Kohrs, pay the wages of the cowboys in full and leave some cash in Jamie's pocket. He still had two hundred cows and calves that would form the basis of his herd.

When they sent the money off to settle the debt with Kohrs, Jamie wrote a letter explaining the situation of Patrick's death and thanking them for the confidence that he had shown in them. Enclosed with that letter Kate attached a long note to Augusta, which concluded in a formal way that the girl thought was appropriate: "I will fondly remember the culture and beauty you created in the middle of the wilderness, and the kindness that you showed me. Love, Katherine Bains."

It was sad to see the cowboys leave; they had been through so much together. Chisholm and most of the others were heading south again. Winter on the northern range was not for them. Josh and Lee liked what they saw of Canada and decided to stay around to see if they could make a go of it. They would remain to help Jamie settle.

For a number of days Jamie, Kate and Billy rode out from their camp exploring the foothills country around Fort Macleod. One afternoon they came up to a stream that meandered around until it joined the Oldman River. There was dogwood along the watercourse and rich rolling grasslands that stretched out to the horizon. In the west the Rocky Mountains glistened in the distance.

Jamie reined his stallion in and looked at the scene for a long time. "This is where I will build my ranch," he said quietly. The others knew him well enough to understand that anything was possible with Jamie Bains.

It was the next day that Kate announced that she intended to go home. Jamie was upset. "Why don't you stay here with me, Kate. You and Billy and I can build this ranch together."

"Maybe someday I'll come back, Jamie, but we've been away from home for almost a year now. I miss our mother and the rest of the family. I've got to go before the snow flies and makes it impossible to travel."

They talked a long time about it, but Kate would not change her mind. She knew that it was only right that Jamie stay in the foothills country. He had found what was good for him, but she was being drawn away. How else could she describe it other than to say that she felt she had to move on.

When Jamie was in town he arranged that Kate would follow a Métis cart driver as far as Batoche, where their sister Meg lived. But time was pressing. The cart driver was leaving the next day.

And so it was that Kate gathered up her things. Jamie gave her some money from the sale of the steers, and the three friends, Billy, Jamie and Kate, rode into Fort Macleod early in the morning. They stood on the main street of town as the cart driver readied his load. Then he prodded his ox with a switch, and the Red River cart began moving slowly out of town with its axle shrieking.

Kate stood beside her buffalo pony until the cart had long disappeared. The three of them chatted, reluctant to see her go, but finally the moment could not be put off any longer.

"We'll write to each other," she said, tears welling up in her eyes.

Her brother hugged her. "Give my love to Mother, and Meg and the boys."

"I will."

"We've ridden a long way together, Kate. I'll miss you." Then her brother smiled in his gentle way.

"I'll miss you, too." She wiped away a tear. "Look after him, Billy. Jamie seems to think that he doesn't need anyone, but he does. He needs your help now."

"I will, Kate. If you ever want to come back, I ... I'll always be here."

"Keep out of trouble, Billy," she added with a smile.

"And Kate, thank you. Thank you for believing in me." Even Billy, once the tough outlaw, wiped away a tear.

Kate was about to swing onto her horse when Billy suddenly kissed her. There was an instant of shock and embarrassment. It was the first kiss for both of them. But then Kate was on her horse and riding out of town after the Métis cart driver before either of them could understand what the kiss meant.

"Goodbye!" she shouted and waved her hand at the two boys.

"Goodbye! Good travelling!" they called after her, and a minute later she had ridden out of town onto the broad prairie that stretched to the east as far as the eye could see.

Other Lorimer Books in the Bains Series:

Shantymen of Cache Lake,
0-88862-090-X Cloth; 0-88862-091-8 Paper

The Last Voyage of the Scotian,
0-88862-112-4 Cloth; 0-88862-113-2 Paper

First Spring on the Grand Banks,
0-88862-220-1 Cloth; 0-88862-221-X Paper

Trouble at Lachine Mill,
0-88862-672-X Cloth; 0-88862-673-8 Paper

Harbour Thieves,
0-88862-746-7 Cloth; 0-88862-113-2 Paper

Danger on the Tracks,
0-88862-872-2 Cloth; 0-88862-833-0 Paper

Prairie Fire!
0-55028-609-9 Cloth; 1-55028-608-0 Paper

Sioux Winter,
1-55028-717-6 Cloth, 1-55028-716-8 Paper

Awards and Prizes Received for the Bains Series:

Canada Council Award for Juvenile Literature, 1975
Vicky Metcalfe Award for Children's Literature, 1984